Eira

*H*is ass is all wrong.

My eyes narrow at the napkin in front of me, my nose scrunching as I try to make out where I messed up in the dim restaurant lighting. Paper napkins aren't the easiest to draw on, especially with a ballpoint pen, so I took my time with every line to ensure perfection. And that's why it's irking me to find his ass all wrong.

I showed up at the bar almost an hour early for my best friend Holly's engagement party—partially because I didn't have time to check out the parking situation before today, and partially because I wanted to get a feel for the place before the party started. After twenty minutes of aimless people-watching, my eyes snagged on a man who made my heart gallop like a herd of wild horses in my chest.

Naturally, my first instinct was to dig through my purse for a pen to draw the mountain of a man who was hijacking every shred of my attention—working shoulders down, because I can't quite make out the details of his face.

All six-foot-whatever, two hundred-plus pounds of him is wearing a navy button-up that tugs across his shoulders, and a pair of slacks tight enough I'm left with no choice but to imagine what he looks like underneath. Plunking an empty pint glass down on the bar top, he runs a hand through dark hair, letting it fall messy and tousled.

My attention shifts from the gorgeous beefcake in front of me to the drawing that's committing him to my memory, and I begin delicately shading the dark hair on his exposed forearm. When I look back up, he's gone.

With a surly exhale, I reach for a piece of bread to dunk in olive oil. The bangles littering my left arm chime together seconds before clanging off the wine glass brimming with water.

"Shit!" I jump out of my seat as the glass shatters across the table, water surging along every thread in the white tablecloth. "Shit, shit, *shit*."

My dress is wet. My phone is wet. The people seated at the surrounding tables are staring. If tonight wasn't my best friend's engagement party, I'd be halfway out the door already.

"Are you okay?" A gruff voice rumbles through me like the vibration of an old steam train.

A man—*the* man; my muse with the great ass—towers over me. Close enough I feel his breath running through my hair as he leans in to grab my phone and wallet, and starts meticulously drying them with his shirtsleeve.

"Yeah. I'm just really wet."

Ope.

Embarrassed heat prickles under my skin, and ass-man shoves my white leather wallet toward me with a small cough. His blessings in the genetics department extend beyond the perfect bubble butt, and I do my best to memorize every detail of his chiseled jaw and intense, azure eyes. It'll take hours to get the five o'clock shadow just right, but that's an endeavour I'm willing to stay up all night for.

And when he leans in to help a server clear the mess, a wave of vanilla and tobacco crashes over me. I'm still tumbling beneath the surf, blissed out in the spicy yet sweet aroma, when his muffled voice snaps me back to reality.

A reality where ass-man is holding a slightly damp piece of paper featuring a somewhat risqué drawing of his physique.

"That's... uh, that's nothing. I'll take that back, thanks." I reach to grab it, but his arm jerks at the last second. Watching

Christmas at Fox Ridge

Bailey Hannah

Cover design by Chelsea Brooke

Editing by Editing by Andrea

Interior artwork (paperback edition) by NudePencil

Print ISBN 978-1-0688647-0-4

eBook ISBN 978-1-0688647-1-1

If you've spent countless hours on farrier TikTok, this one's for you.

Eira: AY-ruh

That's it, that's all. She *hates* when people mess it up.

the twist of judgemental confusion in his dark eyebrows, I feel overwhelmed with the need to add, "We all have butts."

We all have butts?

That was a... *choice.*

He snorts. "That we do."

"Yours doesn't actually have that flat spot, by the way."

Foot, meet mouth. I wish I could say I'm usually more suave than this, but that's wholly untrue.

"This is my butt? Hrmm..." Words falling out the side of his mouth, he gives the limp napkin another cursory glance. "I'd say I'm flattered, but I don't love knowing a beautiful woman thinks my ass looks like that."

"A crappy ballpoint pen isn't exactly the best medium, especially for drawing on a paper napkin. It has everything to do with that, and nothing to do with..." I wave a hand in his direction.

"No, no. Aside from my missing head, this is an amazing drawing. I mean, look at the detail in my shoulder muscles. I refuse to blame this on your artistic abilities." There's a slight flex in his forearm when he twists the paper to show me my illustration—a new level of muscle definition and branched veins that even the world's best artist couldn't replicate. "Leads me to believe the problem is with my pants."

He turns to thank the server for cleaning up my disaster, smoothly sliding a cash tip into the guy's hand. I take a half-second to eye-fuck the ass-man. It's definitely *not* the pants that are the problem here. He could make me sweat wearing a pair of oversized Hello Kitty pajamas.

"So," he says, spinning around to catch me ogling him. "Is it the pants?"

"We-ell." I tip my palms upward with a shrug, playing along with his flirty game. "Pretty hard to tell without knowing what you look like without them."

I'm sorry, who is she?! And where did that come from?

His wide-eyed expression makes a feverish heat crest my cheeks, no doubt turning me a hideous shade of red.

"Should we head to the bathroom over there right now, and I'll strip so you can get my ass just right? You artist types like to work with nude models, don't you?"

I'm both salivating and parched at the prospect of seeing so much as one more inch of bare skin. His fitted pants are pushing me to the edge, forearms about to send me over. Which is probably why I can't keep my mouth shut.

"I actually had mono the week my class in university worked with a nude model."

"Kissing disease the week of the naked dude? Bad luck, Doodlebug. We should consider a makeup class."

I lick my lips, heart shifting from a stilted, nervous thumping to a thunderous slam within my chest. Despite the bile threatening my esophagus and the flush in my cheeks, I say, "I *have* always wanted to try it."

And the burly man just smirks at me. Eyes so big and blue, I'm considering going for a long dip. Maybe I'll drown myself in them.

"I'm Lucas." He holds out the limp napkin, fingertips grazing mine with a symphony of fireworks as I snatch it away.

"Eira," I say, drawing out the *ay*, because I hate when people pronounce it *eye-ruh*.

His brows furrow, and he repeats my name back slowly. It happens all the time when you have an unusual name, but hearing it roll off a man's tongue has never sent warmth through my entire body like this.

"Eira... Are you, by any chance—"

"Eira!" My best friend, Holly, suddenly bounces into view, shouting my name. Sidling up beside me, she pinches the fabric at my waist. "This dress is killer."

"And it doesn't even make my ass look flat." I smooth a hand over my butt cheek, catching the slow drag of Lucas's thick bottom lip between his teeth.

"That remains to be seen," Lucas quips.

Holly rolls her eyes, slinging an arm around the mountain man of my dreams—the man I'm really hoping to see naked in the bathroom shortly. And presumably again later tonight.

"I see you met my pain-in-the-ass brother."

Chapter Two

Eira

Six Months Later

"That's a penis inside a hot dog bun."

"Sure is." I grab my phone from Holly, shoving it in my coat pocket before any innocent souls in this crowded coffee shop become permanently scarred by the bizarro dick pic on my screen. "This is what dating is like now. Don't you miss it?"

"I just..." She takes a slow sip of coffee with a pensive bunching of her eyebrows. "What possessed him to flop his sausage into a hot dog bun and take a photo?"

"Probably wanted to stand out from the countless normal dick pics women on this app receive." I shrug, taking a deep breath of the coffee-scented air.

Holly and I have been regulars at Sipsters every Sunday morning since a roommate mix-up in our first year of university led to us becoming inseparable. Used to be that we came here for breakfast wraps—the ultimate hangover food—and to recap whatever wild shit we did the night before. Now we lament adult life and she manages my online dating profiles, swiping left and right with the occasional pause to confirm whether I like mustaches (I do), or ask what my feelings are on facial piercings (take them or leave them).

"It definitely stands out." Holly's fingernails tap against her mug. "Let me see it again."

With a laugh, I hand over the phone. "You're sick."

She curls up in her oversized armchair, and her fingers spread across the phone screen to zoom in, paying no mind to the patrons milling about behind her who could accidentally look over and get a real eye-full at ten a.m.

"Who *is* this guy, anyway?"

"That firefighter you swiped on. We were supposed to go for dinner last night, but I told him I had a migraine after he sent me that."

Her head tilts for a different angle of the photo, and she squints like she's trying to unlock a secret code. "I bet I can tell you exactly what his dinner plans were. Okay, so what about the guy you went out with on Thursday?"

"*Fuck that guy.*" I take a swig of my coffee, staring across the cafe at a couple who can't take their hands off each other. "The entire time we browsed the menu, he was going on and on about macros. So naturally I stuck to a side salad and then ordered pizza when I got home. Plus, when I mentioned my illustrations, his only question was if I have a 'real job'."

"Fucker." She slides my phone across the table to me and makes a face. "Somebody with as much talent as you doesn't need a blood—*and creativity*—sucking corporate job. Macro-dummy would know that if he bothered to look at them."

I snort. Something tells me showing him my explicit monster smut illustrations wouldn't sway his opinion. "Unfortunately, the bloodsuckers pay well, so I have to tough it out for the foreseeable future."

I do well selling illustrated book covers and character art commissions, even bringing in hundreds of dollars each month through a paid platform where I post NSFW drawings weekly. But as much as it pains me to admit, I doubt I'll be in a place where I'm making enough to pay the bills anytime soon—at least, not if I'm going to keep my $2,500-per-month apartment in the city.

"At least the holidays are coming up, and my vampiric boss is closing the office for a few days."

"Speaking of the holidays, have you figured out what you're going to do for Christmas?"

Tossing my head back with a groan, I slump further down into the chair and look out the window. Piles of off-white snow line the slick city street, and people trudge cautiously down the sidewalk littered with blue de-icing salt.

"Since Mom and Dad are doing a Mediterranean cruise, abandoning their only daughter, I guess I'll sit at home and draw. Hopefully I can make a few pieces to sell on top of my commissions." I shrug casually. "And please don't feel the need to give me yet another pity invite to come to Daniel's parents' house like I'm your pet dog."

I don't *really* care that my parents won't be around. We've never been the type of family to go all out for holidays, anyway. Dad drags the pre-decorated tree up from storage on Christmas Eve, and the three of us eat our weight in food while watching movies. The morning of the twenty-sixth it's back to business as usual. But this year I'll spend the entire holiday season rotting alone in my studio apartment.

"You're our love-child, not dog." She wags a finger. "Actually, I was wondering how you'd feel about renting a cabin in the woods."

I blink at her. Then down at the expensive heeled boots on my feet. Then back at her.

I'm waiting for the punchline.

Seems there isn't one.

"Yeah, no, Holls. I know we're annoyed with my parents for ditching me at Christmas, but I don't think that warrants them coming home to find out their only child died alone in the woods."

"I think the police would contact them on their cruise. They wouldn't have to wait to find out."

"Even worse. Now I'm dead *and* it's ruining their holiday." The last bit of coffee goes down cold. "I'm not sure where you're going with this, but when have I ever given off 'cabin in the woods' vibes?"

"That's why you'd be perfect." *This is a sales pitch.* I know one when I see it. And the way she's leaning forward, steepling her hands and staring into my soul would be a dead giveaway for even the most unobservant. "I've told you before that my brother has a ranch a few hours outside the city, right?"

My stomach rolls at the mention of Lucas, and a vivid slideshow of the night we spent together flashes behind my eyes. Normally, any social engagement leaves me reeling over the things I might've said wrong. All the potential ways I could've embarrassed myself without even knowing it—the moments where somebody quickly changed the subject or pulled a face after something I said.

With Lucas, I embarrassed myself in the worst way, yet didn't have a niggling voice telling me he thought I was a complete loser. I didn't go home and lose sleep replaying every second of our interaction.

Okay, maybe I did... but in a *good* way. No room for self-loathing inside the effervescence of each Lucas-infused thought. His touch branded into my skin, scent ingrained in my memory, and kiss stained on my lips. My mental tape of that night wore out from being played so often.

Sitting at the bar until well past midnight—long after the party guests left and the live band packed up—I drew various bar-patrons on cocktail napkins. Then Lucas guessed who each one was, and we made up absurd backstories for every person we didn't know, constantly trying to outdo one another.

"Terry actually just found out his wife spent their entire life savings on 1990s Beanie Babies," I whispered, punctuating the end with a tipsy hiccup and finishing the details on what had to be my thirtieth napkin drawing. The subject was a lonely looking, middle-aged man wallowing in a concerning amount of cheap vodka at the far end of the bar.

"People have always said they were going to be worth a lot of money one day," Lucas shrugged, finishing the last of his bourbon.

The thought of tasting it on his tongue made my core tighten, and I instinctively licked my lips.

"Maybe that day is coming soon, and she knows something we don't," he said.

I grimaced. "Sure. But at what cost? Terry kicked her out, and she's living in a self-storage unit with 10,000 stuffed animals."

Lucas's empty glass clunked against the bar top, and he undressed me with a heated gaze under the dim bar light as he swallowed. "You should come back to my hotel." A statement rather than a question.

My fingertips teasingly walked the length of his muscular forearm, feigning sultry confidence. "To check out your Beanie Baby collection?"

With a laugh under his breath, he said, "Nothing I plan to do to you tonight is child's play, Eira."

"Earth to Eira." Holly's fingers snap directly in front of my face. "How was La-La-Land? Is Ryan Gosling as dreamy as we think?"

No, but your brother is.

"Sorry." I blink away a fleeting memory of Lucas kissing his way down my body in the dark hotel room. "He's still the hottest of the Ryans. What's the scheme you have planned?"

"So, my brother's ranch. I convinced him to rent out the spare cabin as a vacation rental. Lucas renovated it, and it's gorgeous. Doesn't feel like a cabin in the woods, I promise. Since we'll mostly be renting to city people, and you're... *you*, I thought you might be a good test subject."

"A good test subject for murder?"

"There will be nobody around to murder you." *Just me and him. Alone. In the woods.* "And Luke doesn't exhibit any classic serial killer traits, so I think you're safe. Besides, you're both total homebodies, and he's a complete grump. I bet you won't even see him."

None of that sounds anything like the charismatic, flirty, and funny guy I spent the night with. The mountain man who stole every ounce of my attention all night, who tenderly washed my body in the hotel's walk-in shower after hours of intense sex, and who insisted he order room service before I left the following morning.

"He didn't seem that way at your party," I say.

"You caught him on the *one* night he let loose. He's usually so wrapped up in trying to keep the ranch afloat. And it sucks he's so stressed and irritable all the time, because he's a really sweet guy."

"And having somebody intrude on his personal space over Christmas is going to make him less stressed and irritable?"

"Like I said, you won't even see each other. Spend the holidays there and let me know if anything needs to change to make it more inviting for guests. He hates the idea of having a vacation rental, but I'm hoping the extra income will take some weight off his shoulders."

Okay, if I frame it as being *helpful*, the idea doesn't sound so terrible. Getting out of the city means a few days to work on commissions, unplug from dating apps, and relax. Without distraction, I'd be able to get a lot done.

Sure, Lucas and I hooked up once six months ago, but I'm confident we can be adults about that, on the off-hand chance we see each other from afar.

"There's a gorgeous clawfoot tub big enough you can submerge your entire body," Holly says with a raised eyebrow.

"Well, *fuck*. Now I'm sold."

Chapter Three

Lucas

December 20

Tugging my arm across my chest to stretch out the constant dull ache in my shoulder, I stare down the alley at the final mare for the night. I typically limit myself to working Monday through Thursday—any more and I feel it in my bones for days. But after a rough summer, nasty fall, and the start of what looks to be an abysmal winter, my options are busting my ass for more money or selling the ranch. Which is why I'm working at six p.m. on a Saturday, listening to the wind whip through the rafters of the otherwise silent barn.

I'm *not* selling the ranch.

Don't give a crap what my family thinks.

I give the old mare I just finished trimming a few extra scratches along her back while feeling around in my pocket for a mint. She takes it greedily then politely sniffs my hand for more.

"Sorry, girl. Just one today. Not supposed to give you any, but you know you're my favourite here."

Her withers shudder as I drag my nails down the root of her mane.

I plunk my tools down ten feet away, and a resounding crack carries up my spine. The obnoxious ringer my little sister set for herself echoes through the barn. Frigid air has me creating billowing vapour when I bark out a surly greeting.

"Did you put any more thought into my proposition?" Holly asks immediately.

"No."

"No, you didn't put more thought into it? Or no, you don't want to do it?"

I take a swig of coffee. It was hot when I took a lunch break four hours ago. Now it's disgustingly cold, but I need any jolt of caffeine I can get, so I throw my head back and chug it.

"No to both." Switching the call to speakerphone, I balance the cell precariously on a sawhorse and grab my tools. The sooner I get this horse done, the sooner I can have a hot shower and collapse into bed. The sooner I get up and do this again tomorrow.

"Luke, you came to me bitching about the ranch's finances—"

"*Wrong*," I interrupt. "I talked to your fiancé, because he works in finance, and you decided to involve yourself."

"Same thing. Can you just try it? I already have somebody lined up to stay there over Christmas."

Of course she does.

I groan, giving a nail in the horse's shoe a firm tug. Despite the cold, sweat prickles my back and dots my hairline.

Holly seems to be giddy on the other end of the phone. "Please do this test run before you decide. Having some extra income is going to make a huge difference."

"I'm not dealing with this person at all. I don't want to see them or hear them or anything."

"I've got it all handled. You installed a digital keypad on the door, right?"

"Reluctantly."

"Then you won't even know they're there."

Better fucking not.

"Fine." The horseshoe tugs free, falling to the cement barn floor with a vibrating clang amidst the late-afternoon stillness. "Remind me to never talk to Daniel about anything again."

"You could always sell it, like Mom keeps suggesting. Walk away with a loaded wallet and buy yourself a house in town."

Adjusting the positioning of the mare's pastern on my thigh, I reply, "Hanging up now."

"Love you. Promise this rental plan is going to be great."

* * * * *

Finally pulling up to my own barn, I breathe a small sigh of relief. This place is my solace, and just breathing in the smell of hay, horses, and old wood is enough to remind me why I'm working so fucking hard.

This is all I have.

"What're you still doing here?" I shout to Cora, wherever she is.

She manages my horses, and my bookkeeping, in exchange for free rent in the studio suite above the barn. Despite being just twenty-three, Cora works harder and bitches less than the two grizzled men who oversee the cattle operation. It's especially impressive considering how much extra weight she's been pulling the last few months with my long hours, while also working full time as a kindergarten teacher in town.

"Popcorn cut up his leg on the fence again," she calls back from deeper in the barn.

Shaking my head, I stride down the alley toward her. The barn lights hum in the crisp night air overhead. Sure enough, Cora's knelt down on the cement floor, wrapping his wound in a hot-pink bandage. Her gelding has about as much self-protection instincts as the five-year-olds who named him.

"He's an idiot." I lean back against the cold metal fence rail.

"Or smart enough to know a little cut means he gets to stay in the warm barn."

"*Sure.* Keep telling yourself that." I snort, rapping my knuckles against the fence. "You going home for Christmas?"

"Wow, I knew you were an ass, but considering I poured my heart out about my family issues when we were unloading all that hay last week, I'd expect you to remember."

Shit. Okay, so maybe it's not just that the town thinks I'm an asshole.

Maybe I am *an asshole.*

"No, I fucking remember," I lie. "Thought you might've resolved things."

She pauses, turning to give me a look that calls me out on my bullshit. After tucking the bandage end, she stands and swipes her hands across her thighs, knocking dust into the air. "I didn't. I'm spending Christmas Day with a teacher friend of mine, but I'll still be around to do chores."

With a single nod, I head back toward the large barn door, stopping only for a split second to fork over a mint to my senior mare—the horse who filled my head with dreams about owning property, working with horses, and riding off into sunsets. Her muzzle tickles my palm, and I whisper a good night to her.

❊ ❊ ❊ ❊ ❊

Save for the porch light, the house is dark when I pull up shortly after eight o'clock, and I use the side of my boot to brush snow off each step on my way to the front door. The heavy flapping of an owl's wings briefly fills the night, and it's cold—*fuck me, is it cold*. So cold my frozen fingertips fumble to open the unlocked door handle.

After slipping my boots off next to the wood stove, I turn on a single lamp and make my way to the kitchen for dinner.

"Shit, I need to grab groceries before everything shuts down for Christmas," I mutter to myself, reaching for a box of KD macaroni and cheese on the pantry shelf. When I'm not so exhausted all the time, I do my best to cook healthy meals from scratch. Nothing beats a grain-finished cut of beef on the barbecue, served alongside garden-fresh, roasted vegetables. In fact, my favourite way to decompress is sitting out on the porch with dinner and an ice-cold beer, revelling in the quiet of my ranch.

But lately, it's takeout, Kraft Dinner, or cereal eaten in the wood stove's golden glow while I fight to keep my eyelids propped up long enough to finish.

As I'm lazily standing with my hip propped against the counter, stirring the simmering macaroni, a light in the cabin out back catches my eye. I shift on my feet, angling for a better view. Sure enough, a small black car's parked outside the well-lit cabin.

Fucking Holly.

When she said she had somebody lined up to stay here, she didn't tell me they were coming *today*. She knew all too well I wouldn't be able to say no.

Frankly, having somebody in my empty cabin for two hundred bucks per night will definitely put a dent in the financial crisis I'm in. After a handful of rented nights, I'll be able to buy enough hay for the animals to get through until spring, without the need for a hefty bank loan from Holly's fiancé. If my sister's right, I won't have to see whatever city-slickers stay here, and in theory, the person staying there for the next few days might just be the resolution to all my problems.

I'm only a *little* annoyed that all the lights are on—*mental note: change bulbs out for the power-saving kind.* And after I vetoed paying for an electric baseboard heater, Holly said she'd leave instructions for the wood stove, so I wouldn't need to babysit their heat source. But whoever's in the cabin better not burn through firewood like it's free.

With a huff, I scoop overcooked, neon-orange noodles into a bowl and shut the kitchen blinds for the first time since moving in. I peruse the local paper to keep me awake as I eat, and then my legs struggle to stumble upstairs to shower. The hot water massages my weary muscles and warms my frigid bones. And the last thing I notice before my still-wet head hits the pillow is the bathroom light on in the cabin across the way.

Chapter Four

Eira

December 20

White knuckling the steering wheel, I creep along a snow-covered road surrounded by nothing but trees. In a way, it's akin to the city, where high-rises tower on either side. Both equally claustrophobic and intimidating. I might have to call Holly and let her know I'm holed up here until spring, because the idea of facing this road again makes my palms sweat.

Braking outside a sturdy metal gate, I blindly feel around on the passenger seat for my phone to confirm the address is correct. If I'm going to die out here, I'd rather it not be from my own stupidity, like being shot while accidentally trespassing.

Stepping outside, I take my first breath of frosty mountain air. Ice particles fill my lungs until they hurt in a way that's reminiscent of over-inflating them with helium at elementary school soccer wrap-up parties. My chest aches, and I cough a little as I approach the metal gate.

With a bone-chilling squeal, the gate swings open, and I'm officially on the property.

Lucas McKinney's property, specifically.

But that doesn't matter. He's not what I'm here for. I have a car loaded with groceries, art supplies, and comfy clothes. A cozy log cabin with a bathtub I can stay forever in. And five days of flitting about a quaint cabin, pretending to be Cameron Diaz in *The Holiday*—sans Jude Law, because I'm desperately in need of a break from the dating scene.

* * * * *

I squint down at the instructions from Holly for the fortieth time, shaking my head. When she told me about the wood-stove, a tiny, independent-woman roar sounded in my chest.

I can handle putting a few logs on the fire.

No problem.

By the time I finished lugging my stuff inside—trekking through snow that spilled overtop the cute new Ugg boots I bought for this trip—I was sweating. Cooking a frozen pizza for dinner heated the tiny cabin even more. But shortly after sunset, a deep freeze set in, and my fingers became too frigid to continue my commissioned book cover illustration. And that's when I realized my mistake.

Big problem.

"Fucking Holly," I mutter under my breath, flicking the barbecue lighter and holding the orange flame to a piece of crumpled newspaper until it catches.

Just like every other fucking time, the newspaper burns up in a flash, and there's no sign of fire except a tease of charring on the chunks of wood I stuffed inside the cast iron chamber. I exhale, sinking back on my heels, and shut my eyes to think.

There isn't a single bone in my born-and-bred city girl body that can handle this shit. I fully accept that I won't last a single day in an apocalypse. There was never a moment while reading the *Dear Canada* series as a child when I thought, "Huh, I'd love to live in a different century." I'm built for elec-tricity, candy cane flat whites, the internet, and good skincare products.

And since the world hates me, there's no cell service here. I'm left to fend for myself like an 1800s Protestant spinster, braving the cold in this house alone because no man will find me worthy of marriage now. Twenty-eight, not a virgin. *Shame.*

Okay, maybe that's a touch dramatic.

Anyway...

I can't be cold if I'm submerged to my chin in a piping-hot bath. And since this isn't the 1800s, I have hot water straight from the tap. No fire required.

The bathroom's small but, like the rest of the cabin, it's tastefully renovated. An antique charm still exists in the rich hardwood floors, stunning wood furniture, and muted colours used throughout. It's something I'm sure I've seen on the accounts my friends are constantly reposting on their feeds—the type of influencer who wears linen dresses, collects farm-fresh eggs with a baby on her hip, and bakes sourdough bread.

Thankfully, the tap water turns hot almost instantly, and within minutes, I'm sinking into a bubble bath that thaws my frozen bone marrow.

And that's where I stay. Drawing on my tablet. Reading a book. Staring into space. Refilling with hot water whenever it cools off too much for my liking. Cursing my best friend.

Until sometime hours later, when my eyelids are heavy and every blink is in slow motion, and I reluctantly drag myself from the tub. It's a fight to pull on my clothes, thanks to violently shivering limbs and damp skin.

My teeth chatter, and I grab every clothing item from my suitcase, debating whether it would be best to cut my losses and head home. Soon I'm looking like the younger brother from *A Christmas Story* when he's stuffed into that snowsuit he can barely move in. Multiple pairs of pants, three sweaters, a scarf up to my nose, and a hat pulled as low as I can get it.

And for a few moments, I lie in bed, unable to get comfortable thanks to the four different waistbands creeping up my stomach in a bizarro arms-race.

"Fuck this. I'm waking him up."

The deal was not to bother Lucas, but looking out the window and seeing a truck parked outside has me slipping into my boots without question. There aren't any lights on in the house, but this feels like enough of an emergency to warrant waking him up. After all, it wouldn't be a good look for his new vacation rental to have a girl die on night one—though he'd be able to tap into the ghost hunter and "spooky girl" market, I guess.

Snow swirls around in the wind, and I trudge slowly through dense snow. Absent of a moon, the inky sky provides no light, so I hold my phone out with a shivering grasp to illuminate my path to Lucas's house. The porch stairs groan under my weight, and the light rap on his front door makes my knuckles sting.

The wind has me pawing at loose strands of hair falling over my face, and I inhale sharply through my teeth before knocking again. Harder this time.

Nothing.

I shuffle sideways to peer in the living room window. No lights. No Christmas decorations. No clutter. Nothing. It's as if nobody lives here at all.

When the heel of my hand slamming into the wooden door doesn't garner a response, I groan and turn back toward the cabin.

Then angels sing.

Okay, not quite. But somebody *is* stomping their way downstairs. The yellowed porch light flickers on, temporarily blinding me, and the front door swings open with a gruff, "*What?*"

There he is. Wearing nothing but a pair of charcoal boxer briefs slung low on his hips. Hair disheveled, coarse stubble grown in thick along his jaw, and a snarl on his lip. And as thankful as I am for the opportunity to see him again, this initial reaction to having somebody at his door is *exactly* why I didn't come over earlier.

"It's the middle of the night," he growls, not bothering to look at me as he rubs his eyes. "The hell do you need?"

I tug at the clothes that are suddenly incredibly tight and hot. "Um... The uh... I can't get a fire lit."

Taking me in, he clears his throat, brusque demeanour changing in an instant. "*Doodlebug?* What the—*You're* staying here? Why didn't Holly tell me you're... *Shit,* come inside."

His large palm falls to my arm—not that I can feel it through all the padding—and Lucas tugs me into the warm house. Now we're standing in the small entryway, neither saying a word. His house smells like wood fire and vanilla. Like him. It's cozy, and rustic, and clean.

"So..." I smack my lips. "I didn't mean to bug you. Holly told me to stay out of your hair, but I couldn't get a fire lit, and I took a bath but eventually started falling asleep, and I didn't think you'd want a corpse in your new rental cabin. Also, dying in the bathtub? I know that's how a lot of celebrities go out, but the *last* thing I need is somebody finding me dead and *naked*—likely in the most unflattering angle, too. So I thought you'd rather be woken up once tonight than by my ghost every night for the rest of eternity."

I inhale deeply as my rambling slows.

His eyebrows cinch together. "You've been in the cabin all day without heat? Why didn't you come over here earlier?"

"Holly said you've been stressed, and you didn't want anything to do with your rental guests. So I thought—"

"That doesn't apply to you, Eira." He tugs at my silk scarf, unraveling it from my neck. "You should've known that."

"I didn't want to bother you," I say as Lucas pulls my toque off and tosses it to the floor. My hands smooth over my hair, which I'm sure looks a mess.

"Your presence would never bother me." He shakes his head with a tight smile. "Holly made it seem like there was a stranger staying here."

"She wanted me to act like a regular guest and give her feedback."

He's undressing me slowly. Layer by layer. Unzipping sweaters, unbuttoning pants. Tossing each article of clothing into a heap by the front door. And I just let it happen. I don't even bother asking *why* I'm suddenly in nothing but a pair of leggings and a thin tank. I'm too lost in the rasp of his breathing, my own heavy exhale caught in my throat.

"So far, I have some choice words for her about the wood-stove and the instructions she gave for it."

He laughs under his breath. "I have some choice words for her about keeping it a secret that her friend with the perfect ass was going to be on my property. Alone. So close to my house."

Blood pounds loudly behind my eardrums as Lucas runs his hands down my bare arms, stopping to rub his thumb over the inside of my wrist.

"What's got your pulse racing, Eira?" He smirks down at me, the warmth and closeness of his body igniting a spark between my thighs.

"Just dreading how much work it'll be to put all those clothes back on."

"You don't need to worry about that since you're not going back outside tonight."

"I'm not?" I whisper.

"No. You can have my bed, and I'll crash on the couch. I'll get a fire lit in the cabin before I head to work in the morning."

Oh, God. I really am a major pain in the neck. This is the furthest thing from not bothering him I can get. "Just tell me how to get the fire going, and I'll be out of here. I can't sleep in your bed, Lucas."

He shrugs. "You have before."

"That was different. You invited me there, and we..."

We didn't sleep much.

"I'm inviting you now. The only way I'm going to get any sleep tonight is if I know you're safe and warm." His hand grazes my shoulder as he reaches to turn out the only light—leaving me breathless and yearning in the dark. "And

I really need sleep. *Please* go upstairs and make yourself at home."

My eyes flicker toward the steep stairs. "I don't want to intrude."

"Get upstairs, Eira." With a sudden sternness, Lucas stares me down. His hands find the curve of my hips, settling in and guiding me toward the staircase. "Go on. Get to bed."

"Get inside, Eira," he said with a husky growl as we stood in the open doorway of his hotel room.

He gripped my hips with intent, and a needy whimper burst from my chest at the same moment he pressed me into the backside of the door.

I clawed at his shirt, taking hold of the thin fabric as he peppered my neck and jaw with bourbon-soaked kisses. My hips rocked into his, desperate and not giving a fuck if he knew it, forcing the slow hitch of my dress until the damp part of my panties rode against the bulge in his trousers. And still, it wasn't enough.

When my dress finally hit the floor, Lucas took a step back and cursed. Low and growly. All the playfulness of the evening was gone—replaced with pure, blown-out lust in his deep-set eyes.

"Fucking hell, Eira," he muttered under his breath when my fingers wrapped around his wrist, guiding his touch to the place I needed it most.

Together we watched his hand slip below the lace of my underwear, and he captured my moan in a deep kiss.

Lucas clears his throat, breaking the spell, and I'm suddenly aware of the shortness in my breath.

"I'll be gone to work when you wake up, but I'll have your wood stove going. Or feel free to hang out here."

"Okay, uh... thank you." I start toward the stairs, leaving with one last glance over my shoulder. Wondering if he wants to follow me up to bed as badly as I want him to.

But I can't find it in me to ask. To tell him how often I think about that night, or how it meant more to me than it probably should.

His room's warm and smells like the cologne he wore to the party. I fit myself into the slight dip in his mattress where he must normally sleep, tucking my knees to my chest and burying my face in his pillows.

✳ ✳ ✳ ✳ ✳

The house is quiet, Lucas's bed blanketed in early morning sun, and I sit up with a yawn. The floor's chilly when I pad across the room to his dresser. Even though he said he wouldn't be home, I'm tiptoeing around as if I'll disturb someone. Without second thought, I grab his cologne and spritz a small amount on my wrist. Much like what I saw of his house last night, his room's clean and minimalistic. One photo of his family rests in a tiny frame on top of his dresser, but otherwise there's nothing to sneak a peek at unless I snoop through drawers. And I feel plenty intrusive as it is, so I neatly make the bed and head downstairs to grab my things.

Which is where I find an orange sticky note on the door. One word: Dinner?

Dinner.

Does he want to go out for dinner? Does he want me to make him dinner? I need more context here.

Nibbling at my thumbnail, I pocket the note, grab my clothes, and step out into the brisk mountain air. A deep breath makes my nostrils stick together, and there's a twinge of pain in my lungs. For a moment, I regret ever leaving the warmth of his bed. If I stayed there all day, maybe I could work up the courage to invite him to join me by the time he gets home.

Chapter Five

Eira

December 21

C learly this man knows nothing about me if he's expecting me to make him dinner.

Clearly I know nothing about myself—*or I'm in denial*—because I'm actually trying like hell to make something that'll impress him.

It's not that I'm incapable of cooking, because only a full-on moron would fuck up a basic recipe. But I don't have a cookbook. Or internet. And I brought food for simple girl dinners—charcuterie, cereal, popcorn, grilled cheese.

But soup? That's just vegetables in a broth. Easy peasy.

An hour later, things are chopped and floating around in a pot, and I feel like a goddamn domestic goddess. I untie the apron strings slung over the hips my mother insists on referring to as "childbearing" and grab my iPad and Apple Pencil en route to the plush couch. Before long, the only thing on my mind is cobalt-blue alien penis. And trying to figure out exactly what the author meant by *barbed tip*.

*****

"Shit. Fuck. Shit." My hands sting as I let go of the pot handles, fingers crisped like a batch of breakfast sausages. I was deep in the weeds working on my alien commission when a burning smell sent me reeling toward the stove. And I grabbed the pot before thinking about whether the handles could be hot.

Scowling at my pink hands, I make out faint fingerprints. Which means I'm not burned *too* terribly, and I'll still need to wear gloves when I murder my best friend after this shitshow.

Delicately wrapping a tea towel around the pot lid, I lift it and fill the room with black smoke. Every trace of cottagecore bliss in the air dies alongside the charred carrots and potato sludge.

"*Shit.*" The lid slams back down, and I whirl around to collect my belongings as I mutter like the haggard old spinster I am. "Go to the cabin, she said. You'll get to relax, she said. Everything is so *fucking* simple, she said."

Now I need to go to town to buy a new pot for the cabin *and* figure out a plan B for dinner.

I'm still muttering when my feet slide into my soggy Ugg boots. Still carrying on when I wrap myself up in a coat I know won't suffice in the cold mountain air and the cute silk scarf Lucas laughed under his breath about. Unrelenting even when I slam the cabin door and come face to face with a pretty young girl, staring at me with a sweet smile.

Oh, shit.

That's why Lucas didn't follow me to bed last night. He has a girlfriend. One who looks a little young for him, but we all love a fictional age-gap, so who am I to judge in real life? Especially considering my best dating candidate's weenie barely fills a standard-issue hotdog bun.

She pulls a hand from the pocket of her thick, canvas jacket and waves. I can't make out details of her face, and she's fully bundled up from head to toe, but jealousy rears its ugly head regardless. I just know in my gut she's gorgeous.

Fighting the urge to flip her off, I return the friendly wave then press my fully extended middle finger against the backside of my car door—aimed right at her—as I slowly drive by.

Chapter Six

Lucas

December 21

I t took every ounce of self-control to keep myself out of that bed last night. And again this morning, when I dragged my feet while getting ready for work, stealing glances up the stairs at my closed bedroom door. Imagining her in *my* bed, dark-brown hair splayed over *my* pillow. She was right there. So close, I swear I could hear her soft snores when I held my breath and trained my ears.

Knowing she was on the ranch seemed to dip the clock hands in molasses; fuckers moved so slow, it was painful. I checked my phone every five minutes, praying for an excuse to duck out early, but the only incoming message was from Cora, asking if any of my horses need vet care while she has him coming out to look at Popcorn's leg—we both know she'd have a better idea of what my horses need than I do. The only time I've spent with them lately is their monthly foot trim.

But shortly before five o'clock, I'm finally tossing my tools in my bag, ready to get the hell out of here. So focused on heading to the truck, I completely ignore the goodbye head bob from the stable manager as I stride past. Not that she'll be surprised by my churlish behaviour; I've become a bit of a recluse since moving to Fox Ridge. I have no problem finding work, as the only farrier in town—and a damn good one—but outside of that, nobody bothers me.

It all started when I moved in and started renovations. The hardware store owner recommended his carpenter son, and I fired that moron on the first day because I wasn't paying him to do a shittier job than I'm capable of.

Then my realtor set me up on a horrible blind date, only for me to find out later that my date's father is the local pastor. He wrote a whole sermon about me and everything, which turned the entire congregation against me. Apparently I was the bad guy for leaving early, despite the fact she was essentially wearing a T-shirt that read *Still Hung Up On My Ex*.

But the town's final straw seemed to be when I genuinely didn't notice the 4-H kids hawking tickets for a meat raffle outside the grocery store and I knocked over a six-year-old.

Didn't help that I did all that with a natural scowl on my face and a gruff tone. Girls can be cute with their "resting bitch face," but I'm the resident asshole for the same damn thing.

Anyway, after that I might've leaned into the reputation, because being the town grump meant no guilt-trips to buy raffle tickets, no invites to cheesy local events, and nobody setting me up on blind dates with every unmarried woman in town. Somewhere over the last few years, the line between my grumpy persona and the real Lucas McKinney blurred.

But I'm particularly thankful nobody ever tries to make small talk with me when I stop at the store for dinner supplies. Because being a chatty Fox Ridge local would delay my getting home to Eira.

I mean... not home *to* Eira, as if we're a couple. I mean home to my home. Where Eira is. Where I'm hoping she'll let me cook her dinner. Despite the ache in my bones and soreness in my muscles and exhaustion fogging my mind, I'll happily force myself to stay awake to see her.

I don't know if she ever thinks about the night of Holly and Daniel's engagement party, but it's consumed my thoughts for the last six months. More than once, I considered driving to the city—hoping my sister would give me Eira's address without questioning—then thought better of it. After all, we'd agreed it would only ever be a one-night stand.

Eira's fingers crossed the small Uber back seat to interlace mine, and I realized I'd been holding my breath for most of the five-minute drive.

She could've changed her mind—asked our driver to bring her home—but there we were, slipping out of the car together at my hotel. The city lights shone over her skin, bringing out the blue in her eyes and the glitter across her bare collarbones.

I tucked her against my side, feet falling in sync, and her phone echoed from her purse as we sauntered through the quiet lobby.

"It's Holly," she said, tapping at the screen. "She just wanted to know if I got home okay."

"And?" I raised an eyebrow.

"And I'm safely at home in bed." She glanced up at the illuminated elevator sign, then lifted onto the balls of her feet for a kiss. "No sense involving her when we're just hooking up one time, right?"

"Right." I brushed my words across her plump lips. "Just this once."

Fuck. I've never wanted to take back my words like I did after that. They felt wrong the moment I said them, and regret settled deep into the caverns of my chest when I watched her sleep later that night.

From the moment I saw her sitting quietly, focus knitted into the creases between her eyebrows, a small tick in the corner of her mouth, blissfully unaware of the busy bar scene surrounding her, I wanted to know Eira. Moving closer, I watched the muscles tense in her forearm as she drew. The slow brush of fallen hair behind her ear. When she knocked over her water, it was the opportunity I'd been waiting for.

I bought my ranch on a whim, sight unseen, because there was *something* I couldn't shake. It felt like it was exactly where I needed to be. Like it was the start of forever.

And the only other time I've experienced that threaded pull of fate was when I saw her.

＊ ＊ ＊ ＊ ＊

Something flutters in my chest when I pull onto the ranch and see lights on in my house. Like sunshine cascading over the powdery snow, it pours out of nearly every window and floods my soul.

Five years I've lived here, coming home to a dark, empty house night after night. It never bugged me until this very moment, when the thought of walking inside and seeing her has me chucking the truck door open before I've even put the vehicle in park. Even sullen cowboy-types get butterflies sometimes.

With a hard swallow, I swing open the front door and kick off my boots. I saunter through the empty living room, rounding the corner to the kitchen, eagerly awaiting a glimpse of her. Maybe she's hunched over the kitchen table, drawing.

Empty.

"Huh," I mumble, scrubbing a hand over my beard.

Circling around to the bottom of the stairs, I peer up at my bedroom with hope swirling in my chest. I call out, "Eira?"

Silence.

"Doodlebug? You in here?"

Motherfucking silence.

All that balled-up hope falls to my stomach with a painful thud as I sink into my recliner.

I can't believe I was such an idiot. Of course she isn't here.

I let my own beliefs in fate and forever take over, forgetting we were only supposed to be a one-night stand. That she only showed up on my doorstep last night because she was close to freezing to death.

Like the sorry sack of shit I am, I sit there until the angry growling noises from my stomach are too much to bear. Then I drag my ass to the kitchen and grab a box of cereal.

It's on the short walk to the fridge when I decide to torture myself—really anchor the pain of rejection deep into my gut. I steal a glance toward the cabin.

No lights?

"No car?" I whisper to myself, shuffling to get a better look. "She left?"

All that hungry rumbling in my empty stomach ceases instantly, and I flick off the kitchen light on my way upstairs to shower.

I roll my neck with a pained grunt as the hot water pelts my shoulders. Sticking my head directly under the stream, I shut my eyes and allow my imagination to run wild with imagery of Eira in the shower with me, like the morning after in the hotel, when I fell to my knees under the rain shower head and ate her perfect pussy.

I've been aflame for months, consumed by thoughts of her that leave me desperately clinging to my bedsheets, jerking it until my skin is raw.

My dick's rock hard, but I don't touch it. That's my punishment for not sticking around here long enough to talk to her this morning. I left a goddamn sticky note with one word instead of asking her to have dinner with me like a normal person.

Idiot.

I slam the tap off, angrily wrapping a towel around my waist and brushing my teeth so hard my gums hurt.

Idiot.

Chapter Seven

Lucas

I'm flopped on top of my bed in nothing but a towel when a noise downstairs startles me from my self-loathing stupor, and I frantically scrounge up a pair of sweatpants before heading out to investigate. I'm still adjusting the waistband when I get to the top of the stairwell and look down to see her.

"Eira?"

"Hey," she says with an exasperated exhale, tugging the scarf from her neck. "Sorry for letting myself in. It's so cold out, and I was knocking, but you... uh, must've been in the shower." Her eyes rake over my naked torso, my still-damp chest.

"No need to be sorry." All the insecurity that wormed into my brain during my shower dislodges with her easy smile. "Let me get changed, and I'll be right down. I'm glad you understood my vague note about dinner."

"I wasn't quite sure what it meant, so I tried to make something. But, uh, did you know it's possible to burn soup?" She grimaces, nose scrunching up in the cutest way, and I stifle back a laugh, not wanting to embarrass her. "I had to replace your pot... I grabbed takeout while I was in town."

"Can't go wrong with either of the restaurants in town."

"That's what Holly said when I called her to ask."

Mention of my sister has me scrambling away from the quicksand filled with thoughts about fucking her best friend right there against the front door. As much as I want nothing more than to peel her clothes off and wrap her thighs around my neck like a life preserver.

I shouldn't. Not again.

Right?

Tugging on my cleanest pair of jeans and a shirt free of stains, I reach for the bottle of cologne in my dresser. I honestly never bother to wear it, but it feels like my best shot of making myself appear date-worthy.

Eira's sitting at the kitchen table looking out the window as dancing candlelight flickers over her face. Her dark hair's so much shorter than it was at the engagement party, an inch shy of skimming her shoulders. She's ditched the winter coat since I saw her in the doorway, and a loose shirt exposes her kissable collarbone.

That glimpse of effortless beauty has me hating all five years wasted walking into an empty kitchen. Regretting not getting her number six months ago. Cursing myself for not asking her out on a proper date before I had to leave the city.

Looking at the food she's laid out beautifully on porcelain plates I forgot I own, I crack up. "Chicken tenders and French fries?"

Eira's cheeks turn crimson, smile wavering, and I feel like the world's biggest asshole.

"I can't remember the last time I had good chicken tenders." I pull out the wooden chair opposite hers and sink into it. "Problem with raising cattle is it becomes pretty much all you eat. I can't justify buying chicken when there's half a cow sitting in my deep freezer."

"I wasn't sure what was good, or what you and your girlfriend might like, so I panicked and went with something safe." She grabs a fry, slowly twirling it through a dollop of ketchup on her plate. "Is she joining us?"

A fry lodges itself in my throat, and I cough into my closed fist for what feels like a century while she stares at me.

"Girlfriend?"

Nostrils flaring, she looks me over, clearly checking for signs of deceit. "I saw her here this morning..."

"Cora," I say, as if saying her name explains everything. If anything, the stare turned glare from Eira indicates I've done the opposite. "She's just an employee here. Well... sort of. She lives in the apartment above the barn and works for me in exchange for rent."

"So, you're not..."

"No, we're *definitely* not." I reach for the bottle of bourbon, tipping my chin toward her empty glass to check if she wants it filled. She nods, and I fill it as I continue. "As for what I like, I don't care what I'm having for dinner if I get you as company."

Averting her eyes, she tries to hide a smile while taking a thoughtful sip that relaxes something in her shoulders. And for a few moments, we sit together in comfortable silence.

Finally, she opens her mouth to speak. "You'll be happy to know I managed to keep the wood stove going all day."

Actually, I'd love to know she needed to sleep in my bed again.

Even still, I can't help but smile at how proud she is of herself. "Very impressive."

She flourishes a French fry as she speaks. "I basically role-played as Laura Ingalls Wilder all day, trying to romanticize the idea of being alone in a cabin waiting for Almanzo to come home. That's where the idea to make soup came from. And it was going great until I got too distracted with a commission I'm working on."

"I'm way more of a Charles than an Almanzo. Rugged, handsome, good with my hands. Charles would come home and have a good laugh when Caroline's frazzled over the soup. You need to change it so I'm Charles Ingalls, and you can be Caroline." I bite a piece of breaded chicken matter-of-factly.

"You don't get to barge in and make demands during *my* daydream."

"Caroline's hotter than Laura. You should be happy about the switch."

"All this bossing around, you're starting to sound like Nellie." She shakes her head, throwing back the rest of her bourbon with a small wince.

"Doubt I could pull off her curls."

That makes her laugh. Damn if that's not a sound I want to hear every minute of every day.

"Normally, I wouldn't entertain another second of somebody desecrating my girl, Laura, but I'm very curious why you know so much about *Little House on the Prairie.*"

"Three sisters and a mother. I didn't even know shows about superheroes and dinosaurs existed until middle school." I chuckle. "Plus, my mom read us the entire series as bedtime stories."

"Why aren't you spending Christmas with them?" Eira nudges her empty glass toward me, and I happily pour a couple ounces. "I mean, I know Holly's with Daniel's family, but what about the rest of your family?"

I shrug. "My other sisters have families, so my parents are busy jumping between their houses to see grandkids. And no matter how many times Holly hints at it, I'm never doing Christmas with Daniel's family."

Eira smacks her palm against the table edge. "Do you know they go *running* as a family on Christmas day? I'm not even *walking* on a food holiday unless there's a serial killer after me—even then..." Her hands tip like two sides of a scale, weighing out invisible choices.

"A food holiday?"

"You know"—the liquid in her lowball glass swirls with a slow roll of her wrist—"the holidays where all you do is eat. Christmas, Thanksgiving, Easter. Also known as *no pants* holidays."

I cough into my fist, liquor burning a path into my lungs. "Are you related to Winnie the Pooh? Why is your family pantsless on Christmas?"

Eira's laugh makes the tapered candle between us flicker and sway. If it weren't for that open flame, I'd leap across and kiss her. Taste the bourbon on her lips while I imagine spending this Christmas with her, without pants.

"If you wear a big enough shirt, it's like a dress. And I can eat as much as I want without feeling uncomfortable."

"Whatever this weird Christmas of yours is, sign me up. I'll even lend you a T-shirt to wear as a dress."

Eira and I both take a small gulp of liquor, letting the flirtation in my voice hang like dead air between us.

"Honestly, there should be a law against exercise on Christmas Day. I don't know how Holly deals with her in-laws," she says with a grimace. "If I accidentally marry into a marathon-running family, the only running I'm doing is to the divorce attorney's office."

"It would be a holiday though, so they're closed. Now what do you do?"

"Fake my own death," she deadpans. "It's the only way."

Our hands brush when we reach for the same French fry, creating lightning bolts between us. This feels silly—I've fucked her against a wall before. A finger graze over a plate of food shouldn't make my heart rate run rampant. But it does.

"Why aren't you with your family?" I ask.

"I don't have any siblings, and my parents decided to go on a cruise." She tips her glass in mock salute, golden liquid nearly sloshing over the rim. "And I'm not a runner, but I *am* a sucker. Which is how Holly convinced me to come here, despite the fact that I've never expressed an interest in operating a wood stove, or having zero cell service, or snow. In fact, I've always been morally opposed to those things."

"You're *morally opposed* to snow?" I raise an eyebrow. Can't wait for her reasoning here.

"Yes," she says, glass clunking on the table. "For one, my name means snow in Welsh. It's exhausting having to constantly correct pronunciation or deal with people being like, *'Oooh that sounds so foreign, where are you from?'* and I have to awkwardly tell them I was born and raised here."

"I think it's beautiful," I respond honestly.

"Plus, snow is awful. Would you like me to list the ways snow wreaks havoc on everything?"

"Nah, I work outside. I know all too well. Winter's a pain in the ass. But if you get the chance to go into town again, take a drive past the elementary school and look at the snowmen lining the yard. That's my favourite thing about winter."

"The snowmen?" There's that adorable nose scrunch again. "Fun fact, I've never made a snowman before."

I propel forward, leaning far enough across the table, I can practically taste the bourbon on her breath. "You *haven't?*"

She shakes her head with a small shrug.

Before I know what I'm doing, my chair's scraping across the hardwood and I'm standing, clutching the liquor bottle and my glass while beckoning her to follow.

"Where are we—"

"You've lived in Canada your entire life and *never* made a snowman?"

"No snowmen, snow angels, igloos... basically all snowy activities."

"I think that's illegal, and we're righting your wrongs immediately. Can't risk you getting caught." I hold out her jacket so she can slip her arms in then zip the front for her as she tugs on a toque. The scarf she's been wearing isn't going to cut the cold. I hold it up with an eyebrow raised, ignoring her insistence that it's *cute*, and grab one of my thick wool scarves to wrap around her neck.

"It's dark out, you know," she says, but the realization isn't slowing her down. Soon she's fully bundled, following me into the night.

We both pound back the last bit of liquid in our glasses, and everything about the world is hazy except her. She's in full technicolor, smiling at me with a muted crescent moon at her back, full lips slightly parted and in desperate need of kissing. My gloved hands wring together to fight the urge to grab her arm and drag her into me.

"The snowman?" she asks hoarsely.

Right. The fucking snowman.

"Yeah. So, you start with a small ball, like for a snowball fight, and keep rolling it across the snow until it's big enough."

Squatting down, she packs a ball between her mittens. "I've never been in a snowball fight, either."

"Of course you ha—" My sentence's cut off by a snowball hitting hard in my chest.

The obvious culprit's sitting with a sweet smile on her face, daintily putting together a new ball. Testing my resolve. All I want to do when I see that glimmer of mischief in her eyes is press into her with a brazenness I haven't felt since the hotel elevator. But this is a friendly late-night snowball fight. That's all.

"You're a little shit," I choke out. "Expect payback. You're looking at my family's snowball tournament champion."

With a disgusted look, she lobs another my way. "Family snowball tournament? Suddenly the marathon-running in-laws are sounding more appealing."

"Except violence is frowned upon in running. This is a full-contact sport." I lightly toss a snowball in her direction, and she gawks at me when it explodes across her thigh.

"You mean I could tackle you?" There's a terrifying glimmer in her eyes now. Knees straightening, she brushes powder from her legs.

"You could sure try."

With that, Eira's barrelling toward me in slow motion, held back by the shin-deep powder. And when her palms collide with my chest, I stagger backward, wrapping my arms around her instinctively. Nowhere close to a tackle. But now she's pressed against me. A few errant strands of her hair tickle my nose, her heart slams against mine, and she looks up at me with the sweetest tipsy giggle.

"Oof, big guy. You're built like a brick shithouse."

At that, my head lolls back with a gut-busting laugh. When Eira joins in, I realize this is the best night I've had since... well, since the night at the bar with her. Before that? I'm unsure.

"That was the *worst* tackle I've ever seen."

"Maybe that's exactly what I was going for," she says with a coy smile. She's close enough I'm tempted to press my lips to hers. Find out one way or another if those feelings we had months ago still exist on her end. For a moment, we share airspace, lost in a staring contest. Then she breaks it with the slow lick of her bottom lip. "Shall we continue with the snowman?"

Hesitantly pulling out of my grasp, she gives my arm a quick squeeze and jumps back into the snowman project while I pour more bourbon.

"This'll help you stay warm," I say, handing over the glass.

"That's a myth. But thank you." She takes a quick swig, never taking her eyes off mine.

Side by side, she and I push balls of snow around like we're young kids. At one point, I trip, destroying my hard work, and Eira's laugh carries across the entire ranch. It echoes off the log cabin, and the trees, and my heart.

By the time we're finished, my cheeks are aching from laughter and my nose is entirely frozen. And I've never felt so weightless.

"She's beautiful," Eira says, taking a step back to admire our handiwork—which now also features a carrot nose and Eira's fancy silk scarf.

"Great first snowman, Doodlebug."

"Why Doodlebug?"

I shrug. "Was the first thing that popped into my head after I saw you sitting alone, completely transfixed by your drawing despite the bedlam around you."

"That's how I deal with the chaos." She wanders a few feet away and flops into the crisp powder, laying back to create an angel with the slow sweeping motion of her limbs. "I get anxious in new situations, but drawing gets me out of my head."

A shiver racks my body as I sink down next to her. "I get that... You got me out of my head that night."

She cranes her neck to look at me with a smile. Snowflakes cling to every strand of dark hair peeking out from under her toque, glimmering in the dark. "Lucas, I don't know what—*oh my God*, look at th—"

She cuts her sentence short, pointing up to the sky. Blues and purples and greens dance across a pitch-black backdrop. Ribbons of colour swirling, spreading wide and looping back in on themselves, stretched across the night like an uncoiled slinky—pulling something inside me taut until it's begging to snap. The beautiful Aurora Borealis, and the even more stunning Eira Davies. With icy glitter in her hair, wide-eyed joy on her face, and a hand suddenly gripping mine on the snowy ground.

"That's the most incredible thing I've ever seen." Her free hand curves through the air above us, painting each colourful streak.

"Mmm, I know what can top it," I mumble under my breath, ignoring the colour show and staring at her.

"Hrm?" She allows her eyes to flit to mine before returning to the sky above us.

I clear my throat. "Those are the northern lights. We get pretty great views of them up here."

"Wow. I'd love to try and draw them..." The amount of wonder and wistfulness in her voice makes my chest ache. "You get this all the time?"

"All winter long."

The snow under her crunches as she tips her head to look at me. "I can see why you moved out here."

The sight stole my breath the first winter I spent here. Then I got busy working my ass off to maintain this place, never bothering to stay up late enough to catch a glimpse. It's been years too long. So much time passed, there have been a few times when I've nearly forgotten the reason I moved here in the first place. But lying on the frozen earth with Eira's warmth seeping through my damp glove, I finally feel grateful for this ranch again.

Chapter Eight

Eira

"At least there's no chance you'll accidentally draw a misshapen body part if you're painting a picture of the sky."

"Don't count that out just yet. Clouds look an awful lot like butts sometimes."

"I'm starting to think you're obsessed with butts."

"I draw a lot of smutty artwork for authors. It comes with the territory."

"Smutty artwork?" He rolls to his side, hungry eyes pinning me against the snow. Leaving me in the midst of a battle between fire in my veins and ice on my skin. "Like what?"

My mind instantly flashes to the reverse harem sex scene I finished during my lunch break at work the other day. A full hour spent delicately adding the perfect amount of veins to every cock. All five of them.

"Just... character art for romance books. People like to collect it—especially the stuff that isn't exactly safe for work." I gulp, searching his face for judgement. Despite seeing none, I counter with, "I mean, that's really a *small*, tiny, miniscule part of what I do. I make most of my money with illustrated book covers and cutesy type character art."

"Yet you didn't want to draw me in the hotel room? I'm crushed." He throws himself backward into the snow with a hand clutching his chest.

The watercolour sky swirls around us, and all I want to do is tell him how many times I've drawn him in the months since that night. How often I've poured over the page until the early morning hours, ensuring I don't forget a single detail.

"The hotel room has a notepad and pen on my bedside table," he whispered into my ear as the elevator tipped from floor to floor. "I can't wait for you to draw me like a French girl."

"Lucas," I hissed, eyes darting to the man sharing our confined space. The quote wasn't even right, but that was beside the point. "I'm not doing that."

"Because you'll be too busy riding my cock to draw it?"

Heat flared through my skin, and I elbowed him in the stomach. His small groan against my neck had my thighs clamping together.

With a ding, the doors opened, and our friend evacuated the elevator without another glance in our direction. And I climbed Lucas like a tree before they'd fully shut again. Lips crashing into his, I wrapped my thighs around his waist and relied on his tree-trunk arms to support my weight. He pressed me into the wall, consuming me, his lust for me evident between his legs.

"Fuck. I need it," I keened between frantic kisses, wanting every scrap of fabric between us gone as soon as possible. My fingers tightened around the shirt lapel, and his hands moved to grip my ass to steady us.

I needed to feel him. That exact second. *Not in five floors.*

What kind of asshole books a room on the twenty-fifth floor?

"Lucas," I whined, grinding against him like I was in heat. Any friction. Any touch. That's all I needed to set me over the edge. I'd never been like that with a man before—so hungry for any piece of him I could get.

"Almost there." Hot breath against my skin.

"Almost there," I moaned, finally catching his belt against my clit through the fabric of my dress, inching myself so close

1—

"What do you think?" Lucas's deep voice brings me back to the present.

"Sorry, I didn't..." I press my frozen fingertips to my fiery cheek. "I missed what you said."

"I said your cabin's surrounded by so many trees, and you probably won't have enough feeling in your fingers to sit outside painting. So, if you want to try painting the northern lights, the window next to my wood stove has a great view." He sits up, leaving the perfect imprint of his body behind. The back of his coat's soaked through, and he smiles down at me. "What do you think?"

"Lucas..." My stomach lurches, and I glance over at him just as a snowflake lands on the tip of his long, dark eyelashes. Scrambling, I spring up, breath fogging around my face. "I didn't come here to intrude on you, or make things any more stressful for—"

A huffing laugh clouds the air. "You're the farthest thing from an intrusion. I already told you that last night. Or did exposure to the cold ruin your memory?"

"It could also be from breathing burnt soup fumes earlier." I slam a closed fist dramatically into my chest. "You're saying I could've just sauntered on over the moment I realized I couldn't light a fire?"

"Yes. Exactly."

"*Cool.* The hypothermia on night one was all for nothing. So far, this place is getting a two-star review."

"Close brush with death and still give two stars? Damn, you're easy to please."

My eyes fall to the deep cupid's bow above his upper lip. Then along the stubbled jaw, before winding down his body like the gentle curves of a river. My gaze traipses the landscape and pools in places I need a moment to linger. "Only because the hot ranch owner let me sleep in his bed to make up for it."

"Maybe don't put that in your review."

I shrug. "Would've bumped it to a three if I'd had somebody there with me. You know... for body heat."

"In that case, skin to skin is actually most effective." He sits up, and his hand flexes over his crooked knee. "Damn, I missed this. The back and forth with you."

"You could've called," I say. "I know you didn't have my number but..."

I could've, too.

"Yeah..."

"I could've—*should've*—called you. Your sister keeps trying to set me up with guys, and it's fucking miserable. I've yet to have *half as much* fun as I did with you. Is that pathetic to admit after spending one night together?"

Lucas laughs. Not in a judgemental or malicious manner. He laughs like he understands my exact emotions and has been waiting for the chance to explain them.

"It's probably more pathetic for me to say I've thought about you constantly since then. There's something about you that helps me relax, and I don't get to feel that way often anymore." The waver in his voice makes my heart thump loudly in my chest. Like the protective roar of a wild animal. "A drunk driver hit me seven years ago, and I should've died. I'd always wanted to live somewhere away from the city"—he gestures around us at the sky and thick forest—"and I used my payout to make it happen. But I won't lie and say it hasn't been stressful."

I nod, watching the worry stitch back into the fine lines in his face. It deepens when he pauses to read my expression.

"I've always been a bit impulsive. It's why I hopped on a bull without second thought when offered, why I threw away a sure-fire career at my dad's accounting firm to pursue work as a farrier, why I bought this place based on a few realtor photos because it felt right." The memory elicits a shy smile, and I can feel his soul backing every word. "It's also why I was right there in the bar, about to attempt to woo you with a cheesy pickup line, when you spilled your water."

"You think we were meant to meet that night?"

"Does that sound crazy?"

Maybe a little, in the sense that love at first sight is something I read about, but nobody I know has had it happen in real life. It's always a gradual transition from strangers to friends to something more. One-night stands never make it to the light of morning, and you definitely don't think about them every single night for months afterward.

"No. Granted, we were *technically* meant to meet that night, since Holly orchestrated an entire party for her family and friends to get to know each other." I shiver against the wet running down my spine—snowmelt dripping from the tips of my hair. "But, in the months since, I haven't spent a single second thinking about anybody else from that party."

"Not even my uncle Ted?" He gestures to mimic a massive beard.

"Oh, *yes.* I dream about that majestic beard every night." I fake a swoon. "No, Lucas. Not even him."

"Do you know how many dreams I've had where you show up at my ranch—usually in that little slip of a dress you had on at the party—and I get to feel you under me again? So many fucking dreams of your perfect little pussy, I wake up tasting it." He winces at the last sentence, clearly feeling like he might've crossed a line with the confession. And when I open my mouth to speak, even more words tumble out from between his perfect lips, despite his cheeks becoming redder by the second. "Listen, you're only here for a few days, and it's Christmas, and maybe we could keep each other company rather than retreat to our separate homes. I think I've maybe had a touch too much bourbon, because I know this is a wild proposal, but if you decide you want to do that, I'll leave my front door unlocked. If not, I'll let you enjoy the cabin you rented, and we'll never speak of this moment again."

Then in an instant, his large frame is lumbering back to the house, and I'm shell-shocked in his wake. But fuck me if everything in my body isn't desperate to make chase.

He's right, it's just a few days.

What's the harm?

If we were holding off on hooking up because we didn't want to potentially piss off Holly, that ship sailed six months ago.

Brushing the snow from my back and butt, I glance toward the dark cabin out of obligation. Long enough I can make the argument I considered going back if questioned by the court of Holly. Then I'm jogging my way to Lucas's front porch.

Within seconds of the heavy door slamming shut behind me, he turns the corner from the kitchen with a smile on his face. Already stripped of his coat, his slightly damp T-shirt clings to every curve of his broad upper body. Lucas's massive palms engulf my cheeks, pulling me into a desperate kiss. Tongues intertwining, moans captured between sealed lips, he has me breathless and wanton in his arms.

Layer by layer, he tugs at my wet clothes, peeling them from my skin and letting each article fall to the floor in a series of loud smacks. Until I'm wearing nothing but underwear and a bralette, shivering in his arms despite the heat burning my lungs with every shallow breath. The drag of his tongue down my neck is like the lighting of a match.

My fingers find their way to the hem of his shirt, and I'm lifting to expose his thick torso, firm pecs, broad shoulders. Dark chest hair is matted down from the wet shirt, and his eyes smoulder when he takes in my near-nakedness.

"Come on, baby. Let's warm you up." His lips move over mine while we shuffle across the dimly lit room, neither willing to stop feeling each other up for long enough to walk properly.

The wood stove glows, flooding the surrounding floor and couch with an amber glow, and he lowers me to the plush upholstery. A firm palm splayed over my back, the other cradling my skull, we sink into bliss together. And for a moment, the world falls still, waiting for us to settle into place on his couch.

"We're doing this?" He hovers above me, touching but not *enough*. I need to feel him everywhere. Consuming me.

Maybe I won't spend the holidays working on commissions until my fingers stiffen around the pencil. Maybe I'll spend them with a naked cowboy wrapped around me instead.

Great trade-off, if you ask me.

I nip at his jaw, stubble scraping my lip. "We're doing this."

Not wasting another second, nimble fingers release the bralette clasp at my back in one swift movement. He flings the white lace to the floor and takes my breasts in both hands, massaging and caressing, holding them so he can suck a nipple into his mouth with a sated groan. Then trailing his tongue across my chest to give the same treatment on the other side.

After a moment, Lucas grabs the elastic of my underwear, shimmying it over the curve of my ass and down my goose-bump-covered thighs. There between my legs—my naked body spread before him—he studies me in the dim light. Assessing every curve like he'll mold them from clay. Fingers stippling over each freckle, blemish, and stretch mark with the delicate touch of a sable paint brush. As if he'll be relying on a photographic memory to create a masterpiece later.

Then his palms are ghosting over my skin, leaving me squirming and whimpering as he closes in on the place I need him most. "Please."

"Fuck." He breathes the curse in through gritted teeth. "Don't do that to me. Don't beg like that, or I'm going to lose control."

Naturally, I roll my hips to beg for his touch. "*Pleeeeease.*"

"You're so fucking—" Two digits sinking into my pussy erase the second half of his sentence, both of us letting out a low growl of pleasure. "This pussy. She's driven me insane for the last six months. Do you know that?"

As he pumps into me, the heel of his hand catches on the sensitive bundle of nerves that's begging for attention.

"Show me." The way I move to force him deeper is salacious and insistent. "Show me how insane you've been without me."

A puff of air flares his nostrils, and he smirks before trailing his tongue down past my navel and removing his hand. Fingers sunk into my fleshy hips, he teases me with a slow flick of his tongue over my clit. When I buck, I feel him laugh against my skin. And the jerk moves to lick every inch of skin *except* the place I need.

"I need you. Please. I need—"

He circles my clit, the sensations pulling my body from the couch in a crunch position before I flail backward with a loud cry. I'm the only one who's spent time between my legs in the last six months, and every fantasy was about him, so it makes sense that I'm falling apart mere seconds into feeling his tongue flicker across my pussy.

"This cunt's the best meal I've ever had." He groans against my wet skin, fingers pressing into my outer thighs so he can devour me again. "I've been without it for too long, and I'm fucking starved."

Tongue working me over like it's his job, his hands are left to wander. He cups my breast, sliding my nipples between slightly spread fingers with a reverberating moan. Like a sneeze, pressure builds in my core with every touch and lick and glance up at me. The ache for relief is palpable for only a moment before an orgasm tears through my body, nearly throwing the pair of us from the couch.

"Fuck me," I demand, yanking his face to mine by the root of his hair so I can kiss him and savour the taste of my arousal on his lips.

"I don't... *shit.* I don't have any condoms, baby." His forehead falls to mine with regret. "*Fuck.* I'll get some tomorrow."

"I don't care." The response shocks me, too, and I blink rapidly in disbelief. I wipe the dampness from his beard with a shy smile. "I mean... um, well, I don't care if you don't. I have an IUD. Haven't been with anyone since you."

I hold my breath as my eyes lock on his, silently hoping he can say the same.

"I haven't been with anyone since... or for about five years before that." He gnaws his cheek, breaking eye contact to look down at the wooden floorboards.

"Why?"

"Wasn't interested. But we can always wait until tomorrow, if you want," he says in spite of the way my heels are slowly nudging down the elastic waistband of his boxer briefs. "If I feel that tight pussy of yours riding me with nothing between us, I know I'll be insatiable. I can't guarantee I'll ever be able to go back."

"I don't want to wait."

His thick cock plunges into me without another second of hesitation, stretching me in the most heavenly way. I moan under my breath, spreading my legs wider so he can bottom out with his next thrust. His work-worn hands grab my ankles, moving them to rest on his shoulders while he fills me entirely.

He throws his head back at the same time his hips rock forward. "This pussy is addicting, Eira. One hit after months without it, and I'm ready to throw my fucking life away for another taste."

He's telling me. I can't look at him for fear of doing exactly that. Throwing everything away to stay here, simply so I can have this man all to myself forever.

My nails bite into his forearms to keep me grounded at the same time my back arches to inch me closer to heaven. And seconds before I'm there again, my heart stops and my eyes go wide when everything suddenly lurches to the right.

Toppling.

Sliding.

Whatever you want to call it—falling off the couch while Lucas's cock is buried inside me isn't graceful or pretty.

"Oh my God, are you okay?" He grips my arm, as if he can somehow prevent me from falling further. A look of sheer panic blankets his face. Poor guy probably thought his dick was about to be ripped off.

"My life flashed before my eyes, but I'm okay."

Nothing but pride—and probably the moment—ruined here. Add this scenario to the highlight reel of embarrassing memories for me to replay when I can't sleep in the middle of the night. Heat travels under my skin from my core to my cheeks.

"A full-body blush? Fuck, baby. These perky tits of yours look so sexy in that shade of pink. Matching your pretty pussy."

My nipples tighten under his gaze, and that only adds a lustful glimmer to his eyes. Somehow, he doesn't seem to find me any less sexy than he did before my body crumpled onto his floor.

"Kneel right here, facing the couch. Can't risk you falling again." Lucas presses a palm between my shoulder blades, encouraging my face to fall to the cushion.

Mood not ruined, evidently, since he slips his fingers in his mouth before reaching around to tease my clit. And because it's him, I'm slick and needy again within seconds.

There's a collective moan of sweet relief when he slips back inside. A loving, comforting closeness that lasts a heartbeat. Only long enough for me to look back and watch the shift from soft to feral in his expression.

Then it's damp skin slapping, bruising grip, the occasional slap of his palm over my bare ass. Panting breaths and heaving chests and mussed up hair. His cock slamming into me, stealing the air from my lungs and driving us toward ecstasy.

"Anybody ever played with this pretty little hole, Eira?" His fingertip toys with the delicate skin around my asshole as he thrusts.

I gulp, shaking my head slightly. "No."

"Can I?"

"Y-yes," I say.

Of course he can. Anything. I'll do anything and everything he wants.

Lucas stills inside me, and I hold my breath, waiting for what might come next. A muscle in my thigh trembles out of control, and then suddenly his cock's pulled from between my legs and his teeth sink into my hip.

"Fucking hell." His lips drag over the spot. "Watching your ass jiggle while your pussy squeezes me like that. You're killing me, baby."

"Sorry," I whine.

"Don't you dare apologize for making my dick hard." He slams back into me with a strangled exhale. "Perfect pussy, perfect ass. I'll happily die while filling both."

Spit lands below where his finger's still circling, and he spreads it across my skin while shushing my whimpers. Then his finger prods, delicately pushing inside just enough that I'm arching into the feeling. Wiggling. Needing him deeper.

Just.

Like.

That.

My head lolls with a satiated moan, so full of him it borders on painful.

"That's it. Good girl, taking me in both holes. Does it feel good, baby? Ready for me to move again?"

I nod against the couch cushion, and when he finally moves inside of me, I see nothing but Aurora Borealis behind my eyelids.

Again and again, he sinks every inch into me. Cuss words slip from my mouth so often, they become an incantation. Sweat prickling my lower back, knees burned from the rug under us, I slip a hand to my clit just as the knot in my stomach unravels.

"I can't..." I announce between tremors racking my entire body. "I'm—"

I don't know what I'm about to do, but it feels like a heavy weight on my bladder and, despite the instinct to stop it, his forceful thrusts make me lose all control. I could claw my way out of my own skin with the intensity of pleasure coursing through me.

And at the same moment I float down from heaven, a gush floods down my thighs. There's no way he didn't notice it. Full-body blush is in full effect now, that's for sure.

"So goddamn sexy." Lucas finds a new, unhinged pace, chasing his own high. "Squirting all over my cock like that. *Fuck.*"

With a drawn out final pump, he spills into me. Ideally, I'd stay here forever; having him so close gives the warmth and comfort of a security blanket. Still catching our breath, everything becomes unbearably empty with the slow removal of his body from mine.

"You're seriously a drug, baby. I'm already impatiently waiting for my dick to get hard again so I can be back inside you." His eyes shut as he collapses next to me, entirely blissed out, and I press a soft kiss to his lips.

As much as it pains me, because I'm pretty sure I'm just as addicted, I say, "We've got all week, so you should rest up tonight."

Pulling me into his lap, he kneads the tender skin over my hip where his fingers dug in while he came. "That was the hottest thing I've ever experienced. You soaked me."

I scrunch my nose. "I've never done that before."

"Even better. A Christmas present just for me. Next time, you're doing that on my tongue." His words slur slightly from exhaustion, and before he can insist that it's time for round two, I interlace our fingers and stand. A small tug is all it takes for him to follow.

"You should get some sleep, big guy."

"Come with me." He starts toward the stairs, encouraging me along. "Stay in my bed this week."

"How am I going to give Holly any feedback about the cabin if I'm spending every night in your house?"

"Fuck the cabin. I need you in my bed."

I need that too.

Chapter Nine

Lucas

December 23

T he third alarm ringing throughout the small, dark bedroom makes my temples ache. Reaching through the darkness, I hit snooze with a groan.

There is no way it's already morning.

Fucking hell, six o'clock comes fast when you stay up until after midnight. Granted, I couldn't fathom heading off to bed alone—not with Eira sitting in my living room window, wrapped snug in a red plaid blanket, using watercolour to create a replica of the northern lights in her sketchpad. Especially not after spending the past two days at work, itching for the moment I'd get to come home to see her.

So once we'd finished dinner—and *dessert* spread over the kitchen table—I sat quietly on the couch and watched her work. The way she'd tilt her head to catch the coloured streaks disappearing over the rooftop above her, and the squint as she worked in almost complete darkness. She giggled about the possibility of all the colours on her page running together into one big blob, but when we turned the lights back on, she held up the most stunning painting I've ever seen.

No man in his right mind would go to bed and miss all that.

And now I'm paying for it.

A few weeks ago, I was annoyed that the holidays were forcing me to take time off. Despite my willingness to work—not even demanding extra pay to make up for working

on a holiday—nobody but me seemed to think it was appro-
priate for a farrier to shoe horses on Christmas.

Now? I'm fucking counting down to the end of the work
week. Begging for two days of nothing but Eira. I hope we
don't even leave the bed.

After practically throwing my phone on the fourth alarm,
I run my fingers along the arm she has slung over my chest.
She grumbles something about the annoying ringing sound
under her breath, snuggling in closer, and my nose finds its
way into her silky hair. Somehow, her scent fills me with the
same emotion Christmas made me feel as a kid. Cookies and
a warm early morning by the fire. Ineffable happiness and
wonder.

God, now I really do sound insane.

Seven years ago was the worst year of my life—a drunk
driver nearly killed me on my way home from a rodeo, and
it was six months before I was walking again. For a long while,
hearing people's assurance that "things happen for a reason"
had me picking up a bottle of liquor, not knowing if I was going
to drink it or hit them upside the head. Either way, one of us
was blacking out.

Eventually, the notion grew on me. *Amor fati.*

Trusting in something bigger than myself—and bigger than
the asshole who hit me with his one-tonne pickup—made
the mental and physical pain a little easier to stomach. I just
needed to find the *reason* for the shitty hand I'd been dealt.

That reason was this ranch, which I bought five years ago
with the payout I received from the accident. Since then, I've
poured every ounce of energy into this dream—renovating,
raising animals, farrier work. It gave me purpose.

Aside from that rough first date with the pastor's daughter,
I haven't so much as looked at a woman. No time nor desire.
Like everything else, I took to believing I hadn't found *the one*
for a reason.

Despite insisting things were too busy for me to head to the city for a weekend, I couldn't get out of attending Holly and Daniel's engagement party. And there she was.

Sleek dark hair framed her face as she bent over something on the table, and she remained entirely oblivious to all the madness happening around her. She didn't flinch when a server dropped a tray of drinks. Didn't so much as fumble her pen when a large man bumped into her chair. She was writing or drawing something that seemed important, and aside from her tongue darting out to lick her lips occasionally, the only part of her in motion was her hand. I was mesmerized.

I needed to know her.

Finding out she was my kid sister's best friend probably should've deterred me. And I'm sure it would have, if hours of talking to Eira didn't settle the noise inside my head for the first time in years. That felt too much like fate for me to ignore.

"Don't go," she grumbles when I pull my arm out from under her on the fifth alarm. Something in my chest seizes like an old truck motor.

"I gotta get to work, Doodlebug." I tuck the comforter around her, swallowing hard. "Fuck, I don't want to, though."

"*Please, Lucas,*" she whines.

My hand scrubs my jaw. "You know I can't stand it when you beg."

Rolling onto her back, she reaches out to grab my wrist with a sleepy, crooked smile. "Please."

Motherfucker.

She's batting her eyelashes, discreetly pulling me toward her. Eira knows exactly what she's doing to me. And how easily it's working.

She guides my touch to her thigh.

"*Needy girl.* If I slip my hand between your thighs, I won't be able to control myself. If I touch that beautiful pussy, and she coats my fingers in your wetness, I won't be able to control myself." I groan—her hold tightening, drawing me closer to her heat. I'm already running late and can't afford to skip work, no matter how sore my body is and how desperate I am to be in bed with her. But I simply moan, leaning into her firm pull.

She drags my fingertips up her pussy, biting her lip as she watches. "Losing control yet?"

"Don't do this to me, baby. I'm so fucking pathetic for you."

"How pathetic?" She smiles innocently, like she's not pushing my fingers deep inside her wet cunt. Her ass lifts off the sheets, forcing my touch, dragging the heel of my hand over her clit.

"You make me pick between you and work, I'll be flat broke and homeless real quick."

A whole lot of ugly truth for six o'clock in the morning.

Two nights sharing a bed with this woman, and I'm a simpering wreck.

Out of nowhere, her fingers unfurl from around my forearm. "Guess you better get to work."

Leaving me with glistening fingers and a rock-hard dick, Eira sashays into the bathroom. Every step swings her hips and jiggles her bare ass, until regret seeps out of my pores in the form of cold sweat. And the sound of her starting the shower may as well be a splash of water to the face. Something to wake me from this stupor.

Fuck work.

I stalk across the floorboards, letting them creak and groan as a warning of my approach.

"Eira, *fuck*." My booming voice causes dust to fall from the rafters. This house has clearly been lifeless for too damn long if a little appreciation for my girl has it shaking in its boots.

When the door swings open, Eira's eyes snap to meet mine in the condensation-coated mirror. "Don't you have important cowboy shit to do?"

"Yeah," I growl, moving across the bathroom until I'm practically on top of her. "I do. Like making sure I fuck my snow angel so well her pussy aches all day."

She smirks. "*So pathetic.*"

The shower door swings open, steam billowing out around her. And before I lose sight of Eira behind the fogged-up glass, I'm stepping in after her. Crowding her space, I'm barely breathing as my lips brush over hers and my dick slips between her wet legs. The tip glides over her skin, eliciting a whimper when it nudges her clit. I need her in the *worst* fucking way.

The corner ledge is meant for shampoo bottles or a woman to prop a foot up while she shaves her legs. It's about enough room for half a butt cheek, but I make the best of it, getting just enough support for my squatted position that I feel comfortable beckoning her over.

"Sit on it, baby." My cock twitches against my stomach. I reach out to wrap a hand around her wrist. "Sink that tight cunt down on my cock."

"I thought you had to go to work." She massages her breasts under the stream of water, taunting me. "You should probably get going. Wouldn't want you to be late."

"I don't give a fuck how late I am. Quit being such a fucking tease."

Bending, she kisses me and strokes a wet palm down my shaft. Then roughly cups my balls while smiling against my lips. Her tongue swipes up my jawline, hand massaging between my legs.

She has me by the balls. Figuratively and literally speaking.

Pulling away from where she's nibbling my ear, she spins around and sinks down on my cock before I even get the chance to prepare myself for the sensation of her warmth gripping every inch, tightening when she bottoms out on my lap. A ragged, wall-shaking moan barrels out of my chest, and I drive upward instinctively.

"*Fuck*." I grab her waist. "You're so goddamn tight. See how good it feels when you're a good girl, giving your man this perfect little pussy like he asked for?"

She bounces on my lap while whimpers and moans hang suspended in the socked in, humid shower. Her head dips back, letting drops of water fall from the tips of her dark bob.

And I sink my teeth into her shoulder, close to coming apart thanks to the sound of slapping wet skin and the ripple of her ass with every drop into my lap.

"Lucas." Her voice shakes as she pulls in a breath. "It feels so good."

"So good," I mumble agreement into her wet hair. "You're doing so fucking well, my perfect snow angel."

She's squeezing me in tight, rolling bursts, each one making grunts and groans slip from between my lips.

"Never want this to end," I say. Restless hands run up and down the deep curve of her waist, and a sense of loss washes over me.

I don't want her to go home in a few days.

"Oh my God," she cries out, pussy pulling at my cock, filling my veins with liquid fire. And she falls apart beautifully on my lap, looking over her shoulder at me with pink, bitten lips and a hooded gaze.

I move her up and down my shaft despite the trembling in her thighs. Wrapping an arm around her, I hold tight to ground myself as pleasure licks up my spine, and I'm stuttering curse words against her neck when my own release floods out of me.

Then we sit, cloaked in thick, warm fog. My cock still fully seated inside her warmth, and her head resting on my shoulder. Unrestrained, my heart pounds against her back, and her shallow breathing slowly evens out as her fingertips follow the branching veins on my forearm. I press my lips to her temple.

We could stay like this. I could skip work and keep Eira's skin on mine all day.

A blaring, obnoxious sound kills the mood. The end of my billionth alarm snooze this morning, no doubt.

"You should probably go to work for real," Eira whispers. She doesn't bother trying to hide her feelings. She wants to stay like this, too.

"I should..." My reply is weak and unconvincing. "You could come... if you want. Should only be busy for a couple hours today."

"Don't you like... put shoes on horses?"

I chuckle. "Yeah, that's part of what I do."

"Horses scare the ever-loving shit out of me."

"As long as you don't smuggle any carrots in your pockets, I think you'll be fine."

She grins, tilting her head slightly to catch my eye. "No carrots. But I do currently have an eggplant in my vagina."

I snort a laugh, and my head falls to knock against hers. Her giggles make her pussy clench around my cock until the sharp jolts of electricity under my skin have me forcing her off my lap against my will.

"You're something else," I say when our laughter has died down.

Eira's head tips back to wet her hair, eyes drifting closed, and I'm patiently waiting with a shampoo bottle when she straightens. Every moment of hers feels poetic and grace-ful—from the methodical way she lathers suds across her scalp to the roll of her neck when she rinses them away.

"Okay, I'll come with you." She licks a bead of water from her upper lip. Her arms wrap around my neck, and I pull her in close under the steady flow of hot water. "But I'm sacrificing you and your eggplant to save myself, if it comes down to it."

"I promise I'll keep you safe from those super dangerous horses down at the therapeutic riding stables." I laugh, skim-ming my hands across her waist as we trade positions under the shower stream. "They're used for riding lessons for kids with disabilities, but I'm sure they've secretly been saving all their hostile energy for the day you show up."

"Probably. Horses are notoriously shady bitches."

＊＊＊＊＊

"I know we don't know each other very well yet, but I think I gave you the wrong impression." Eira stands next to my truck, shivering as she watches me lower the tailgate and grab my tools. "Remember when I told you I'm morally opposed to snow? Those feelings extend to cold, outside, dirt...*horse poop.*"

"You're saying you prefer city filth to a little manure?" I laugh, slamming the tailgate and motioning for her to follow me toward the barn. "Do you know how much human shit there probably is all over the city?"

"That's why I don't go to the park," she states, tugging her sleeves down over her hands. She had no clothing cut out for a frozen December day, but she looks distractingly adorable in a pair of my overalls and my Carhartt coat—like a little kid playing dress up.

"Baby, I'll grab you a *clean* blanket from my truck so you aren't sitting on a dirty chair. We'll make you a hot cup of coffee and set you up next to the propane heater so you can draw comfortably."

Maybe it was a mistake inviting her to tag along. I'm well aware she's not a country girl, and even agreeing to stay in a cabin on my property was probably out of her comfort zone. But selfishly, I want to spend as much time as I can with her, knowing we only have a few days.

She follows me inside and pauses as I set down my things. The lights hum through the rafters, and a horse whinnies somewhere a few stalls away. Unsurprisingly, with it being December twenty-third and all, there doesn't seem to be a soul around. In fact, I didn't even notice any other vehicles parked outside.

"Okay, it's actually pretty cute here." She homes in on a row of tacked-up drawings, likely done by the kids who ride here. "Even if it smells like horses."

"Yeah, they did some renovations a couple years back." I take her hand in mine, leading her into a small lunchroom, on the off-hand somebody actually is lurking around. And when the door shuts behind us, I grab the pockets of the thick canvas jacket swallowing her petite frame and crash my lips into hers.

In an alternate universe, I imagine Eira living in Fox Ridge, driving out to bring me coffee while I work, and kissing anytime we want to.

"What was that for?" Her mouth curves into a slight smile.

"Wanted to."

A soft peck. "Good. I want you to want to do that all the time."

"Oh, baby. That's dangerous. I might never stop kissing you, then, because it's already all I want to do."

The way she slowly sucks my bottom lip into her mouth, the seductive tangle of tongues, the hint of spearmint toothpaste on her breath. No surprise it's all I want to do. If I'm sure of anything in life, it's that my lips were designed to be connected to hers as often as possible.

A shiver wrenches her body from mine, and she blinks up sweetly at me. "You said something about hot coffee?"

"Coming right up." I kiss the tip of her nose before letting her fall from my grasp. The can of coffee grounds slides across the countertop, and I dump it into the coffeemaker while stealing glances at her in my periphery.

Sidling up next to me, she takes the canister from my hand and smiles at the label. "That's the coffee I remember my grandpa drinking—he lived with us for a couple years after my grandma died. Didn't even think it still existed."

"Still exists. Still the best coffee you can get."

She pries the lid off and inhales the aroma. "Mmmm. Even without trying your coffee, I can safely say the candy cane flat white from Sipsters is better. When they discontinue it every January, I have dreams about it for months."

I lean against the counter and shake my head. "I know what those words mean separately, but I have no fucking clue what kind of drink that is."

"I don't know what's in it either," she says through a soft laugh. "All I care about is that it tastes like Christmas in a cup. But like, the perfect Christmas you only see in movies, with a real tree, and table full of baked goods, and a crackling fire. The type of Christmas I always dreamed about having when I was growing up."

I raise an eyebrow, my mind reeling with ways I can bring her vision together. The hardest part will be the baking, because the burnt soup doesn't inspire confidence in me that Eira can bake—we'll have to hope the local bakery has stock left.

"You know what's crazy?" I ask.

Plunking the coffee can down on the counter, she looks at me with confusion.

"That sounds *exactly* like the kind of Christmas I have on the ranch."

Chapter Ten

Eira

D espite the *okay* coffee, the chill in the air, and the baggy clothing I'm swimming in, I'm actually enjoying sitting in the barn while he works. At first, I did nothing but watch him—mesmerized by his gentle way with the horses, intrigued by the finesse in his work, and turned on by the near-constant flexing of his arm and shoulder muscles under his thermal long sleeve.

Eventually, I reached for my art bag, wanting to get back to the cover I haven't so much as thought about since the soup burning incident. But the sexy cowboy swinging a heavy hammer, pounding a horseshoe into the perfect shape to fit the horse's foot, was incredibly distracting.

So I opened my drawing pad to a new blank sheet and began my sketch. No tablet with fancy graphic art tools—just pencil scratching over thick paper. Losing myself in every detail of him, no different than that night at the bar. Only this time, it's in a new light, because he looks completely at peace here. He's lost himself, too. He's humming something and talking to the horse, going through the motions with ease. Finishing up, he sets the horse's hoof down and runs a hand over its sleek back. He pauses to untangle a knot in the mane with his fingers then pulls something small from his pocket and feeds it to the animal.

When I was seven, my parents brought me to see the horses they use for carriage rides in the park, and I was *thrilled*. I wore my favourite poofy princess dress, plastic heels, and a tiara—fully expecting somebody to see me riding in a horse-drawn carriage and genuinely believe I was royalty.

But that's not what happened.

Instead, my mom insisted I take a photo with the horses first. Nobody told us one of them hated kids, and I got to learn the hard way that horse bites fucking *hurt*. I cried, my dad yelled at the employees, we didn't take a carriage ride, and my ripped dress was trashed the moment we got home.

"One more, and we can get out of here." Lucas smiles at me, opening a stall door with a bone-chilling squeal.

"Take your time. I'm enjoying this, actually," I reply honestly. Closing my drawing pad to hide the work-in-progress, I stand to stretch. My back cracks, and I raise my arms overhead until the tightness in my shoulders dissipates. "I'm gonna go look around outside."

"Watch out for horse poop," he says with a wink and a smile.

"That's something you never need to remind me of. I'll be on high alert." I push open the door, squinting against the morning sun, and I inhale so much fresh air it makes my lungs ache.

Taking slow, calculated steps so as not to step in anything questionable—though these Uggs are getting thrown out when I get home regardless—I walk around the side of the barn and am met by the most insanely gorgeous view I've ever seen. Sprawling fields blanketed in untouched, white snow. Distant trees and mountains provide small patches of colour amongst the vast ivory earth.

Just as I'm searching in the deep pockets of my overalls for my phone, the tiniest whimpering cry stops me in my tracks.

I swear the breeze, and the clanging of metal in the barn, and the distant horses all still in unison. The world's so quiet, I can hear blood pumping past my eardrums.

The tiny sound rings out again, and I follow it until I find myself next to some sort of wood shed. The cries are undeniably coming from underneath it. Scrunching my nose, I pull out my phone and turn on the flashlight before dropping to my knees next to a hole that's been dug under the shed.

"Hey, whatever's in there, if you could *please* not launch out at my face, that would be great," I call out, as if the critter inside understands me.

Pulse racing, I gulp and move closer.

An emphatic meow.

"Oh, you're a cat!" I laugh a little to myself, thankful I'm not over here pestering a badger or some shit. Quieting my voice so as not to startle it, I attempt to call it out from its hiding spot. "*Pspspspsps.* Come here, kitty. Are you stuck under there?"

My flashlight catches on something, and I slide on my belly across the snow for a better view. Tucked at the far back, with fur plastered to its wet body, looking scared and much too small to be alone, is a tiny kitten.

"Come here, baby." Against better judgement, ignoring the possibility of what else could be in the hole, I shove my hand in to grab the kitten. Falling short, I curse under my breath.

I gnaw at my cheek for a moment, then push up to my feet, announcing that I'll be right back as I quickly shuffle away.

"Hey, do you have any cat food or something here?" I ask, storming into the barn.

Lucas looks up from his work, and confusion washes over his face. "Why are you so wet? Did you slip out there?"

I flap my hand to indicate to him that my current state doesn't matter right now. "I was lying in the snow. Maybe some lunch meat in the fridge or something?"

"Making snow angels again?"

"Trying to rescue a kitten from under a wood shed." Clearly, he's not going to answer my question, so I head for the lunch-room to look for anything I can use as kitten bait.

Lucas is hot on my heels, abandoning the horse he was in the middle of shoeing. "A kitten? Show me."

I lead him out to the shed, half-listening as he rambles about the number of barn cats, and how the kitten is probably perfectly fine where it is.

That is, until he drops to his stomach and peers under the shed.

"Well, Doodlebug. I think you're right. That thing looks pretty small to be out here without its mama." He furrows his eyebrows in thought as he stands back up. "You sure you didn't see an adult cat around here at all?"

"Nope. If she was around, wouldn't she come back when she heard her baby crying?"

"Eira, this might be a case for us to just let nature take its course..."

My jaw goes slack, and I stare at him with a burning sensation behind my eyes. Blinking back tears, I say, "We can't just leave her to die. That's inhumane."

"Well..." He sighs and drags a hand down his face.

"Come here, baby," I say to the kitten, crouching down and rubbing my fingers together in front of the hole, hoping to entice her out. Ignoring Lucas altogether. "Come on out. Promise I'll take good care of you."

Lucas grunts, walking away. And I swear to God, I will never speak to that man for as long as I live after this.

Tears prick my eyelash line, and I lie back down on the cold, compact snow. Like a strong, independent woman, I mutter some curse words about stupid men and get back to work trying to save the kitten. My shoulder's pressed so hard against the shed wall, I'm afraid something might break, and my outstretched fingertips are barely able to stroke the kitten's fur. Nowhere near enough reach to grab it.

I shuffle away from the shed with an exasperated, "Fuck."

"Think cheese will work?" Lucas's voice makes me jump, and suddenly he's next to me, holding a slice of Kraft cheese.

Like a strong, independent woman, I silently admit that I can use some help. Sitting back, I watch as he unwraps it and breaks off a piece, tossing it just inside the hole—close enough I can scoop up the kitten when she takes the bait.

"I hope it does," I whisper.

Then we back off, the sun warming our backs despite the snow slowly soaking through our pants. Silently waiting for the kitten I'm still not sure he gives a shit about.

"That was really harsh of me," he finally says. "I didn't mean I think the cat should *die*. It's just the way things work on a farm sometimes."

I nod solemnly, not taking my eyes off the piece of orange cheese.

"We'll get it, okay? Even if I have to tear the floorboards out of this shed." He takes my hand in his, rubbing a thumb slowly over my skin. "You have dirt—likely some horse poop, too—under your fingernails, and you're sitting on the ground trying to rescue a filthy kitten. I can't exactly ignore that crazy amount of character development."

My lip quirks. "Helpless little animals are my kryptonite. When I was really young, I wanted to be a vet. After a horse bit me, I thought my dreams were crushed entirely, but my grandpa assured me I could be a small animal vet."

He tips his head to look at my face. "Lots to unpack here. *You* wanted to be a vet? Until a *horse* bit you?"

"Yeah. Asshole got me right on the shoulder and ripped my Cinderella dress." I point to the spot, letting my gaze drift from the cheese for half a second to look at him. "I realized later on that I don't have what it takes to be a veterinarian, anyway. But I *did* volunteer at a shelter through high school. Just because I'm not outdoorsy and like to wear cute clothes doesn't mean I can't get my hands dirty when I have to."

"You continuously impress me, you know that?"

Whether he's being genuine or trying to kiss my ass, I don't care right now. I just want the cat to be safe. "Think the cheese will work?"

He purses his lips and leans over to look into the hole. "I hoped it would, but I think she's too scared. But maybe I can—"

With a grunt, he flops to his stomach and shimmies forward, trying and failing to shove his thick arm in the small hole. With a shake of his head, he yanks his coat off and tries again.

"I think... I might..." The crease between his eyebrows tightens. "Fuck. I'm so fucking close—*ouch*! *Bastard.*"

He rockets out of the hole and examines his fingers. "Fucker bit me."

With a snorting laugh, I bury my face into the thick sleeve of my coat.

"It hurt," Lucas whines. "This little shit needs to come out of there right now. I'm gonna show it who's boss."

"Oh, yeah, you're really giving boss energy crying about a tiny kitten bite that didn't even break the skin."

Ignoring me, he crams his hand back in and seconds later exclaims, "Gotcha!"

The tiny, black kitten, clearly scared out of her mind, emits the most non-threatening hiss. She fits perfectly in Lucas's palm, and I beam at him when I scoop her up.

"Poor little girl," I tuck her against my chest and stand. "We'll have to get you some food, and give you a bath, and make sure you're healthy."

"How do you know it's a girl?" Lucas brushes the snow and dirt from his chest.

"I can just sense it, okay? Mother's intuition."

Back in the barn, I curl up on my chair near where Lucas abandoned his work to help me, tucking the blanket around the small cat. The distraught mews slow as she settles in, and a moment later, Lucas appears with a big box.

"I got this so she can't run away, in case you need to set her down." Crouching in front of me, he gives a thin-lipped smile. "She seems old enough to not need milk, which is good. We can grab some wet food at the grocery store on our way home."

I stroke my index finger over her furry head and glance down at the box.

"I know you're still mad about what I said out there. I'm sorry." He seems earnest, with moody eyes and worry knitted in the space around them.

"Volunteering in the shelter, I saw *so many* helpless animals go on to be euthanized. That's when I decided I couldn't be a vet," I say.

"I would've torn that shed to pieces—*carefully*, so the kitten didn't get hurt—if I needed to. We got her, and we'll make sure she's taken care of now. There's a really great animal rescue in town." He lets out a loud exhale, hooking a thumb toward the tied-up horse. "I'm almost done here. We'll give 'em a call after."

Cradling the cat in the crook of my arm, I bring my free hand to the nape of his neck and kiss him.

✳✳✳✳✳

As he loaded his tools back into the truck, I attempted to contact the rescue he'd mentioned. I guess without decorations or presents or family around, we both forgot that tomorrow's Christmas Eve, so naturally, the rescue has its phones off until the new year. But after a lot of eyelash batting, Lucas agreed to keep the kitten until January, even though I'm leaving on Boxing Day.

After finishing up at the barn, both of us had stops to make in town, so Lucas parked his truck on the town's main strip, and we agreed to meet back there in ten minutes. I slipped the kitten in my coat pocket—*thank God men's clothing always has such big pockets*—and held a palm over her tiny body, heading for the small grocery store.

Speed walking, I crane my neck to see down every aisle in search of cat food, thankful for the obnoxiously loud 2000s pop music blasting through the store speakers. There's no way my pocket isn't meowing, given how hungry the animal inside it must be, but if I can't hear it, neither can anybody else.

When my body crashes into somebody, I cuss under my breath and tighten my grip on the kitten.

"Oh, I'm sorry!" the woman says, gripping my upper arm instinctively to stabilize both of us.

"No, I'm sorry. I wasn't paying atten—hey, Cora, right?" I smile at the woman, instantly recognizing her from Lucas's front porch. My hunch was correct: she's stunning.

"Yeah." She nods slowly, eyes narrowed as she tries to figure out who I am. Then a flash of recognition sparks. "*Right*, you're the person staying in the rental cabin at the McKinney Ranch."

Staying at the McKinney Ranch? Yes. In the cabin? Not so much.

"I'm Eira." I reach to shake her hand with my kitten-less one, suddenly aware that she looks gorgeous and I'm covered in any number of disgusting things, hair probably a mess since I left my toque in the truck, and I'm wearing clothes that are way too big for me. Lucas had to roll the bottom of the pants up five times this morning.

"So nice to meet you. How are you liking the cabin? The owner, Lucas, put a lot of work into renovating that place."

"Beautiful place. The wood stove is a nightmare, though."

She laughs. "If it gives you more trouble, I live in the apartment above the barn. Feel free to come find me, rather than Lucas. He's growly and unwelcoming at the best of times."

The same Lucas who insisted I sleep in his bed when I didn't have heat? And who dragged me outside to make a late-night snowman?

I make a face. "He, uh... he already came over to light the stove for me once, actually."

"Okay, damn," she says with a surprised expression. "Must've caught him on a good day. His sister set this whole rental thing up, and he swore up and down he wouldn't have anything to do with people staying there."

"I'm best friends with his sister, so we... have a history, I guess. I'm not a total stranger on his property."

"That makes sense," she says slowly, suddenly eyeballing the heck out of the clothes I'm wearing, possibly questioning who they belong to.

"Anyway, I'm in a bit of a rush. Sorry for running into you, *literally*. It was really great to meet you, though." I skirt past her and rush down the nearest aisle, pleasantly surprised to find it's exactly where the pet supplies are.

Basket loaded with enough cat food to probably last two months, I meander my way toward the check out.

"Is that a cat in your pocket, or are you happy to see me?" Lucas's breath blows hot behind my ear, making my cheeks warm.

"I know two pussies who are pretty happy to see you."

He grabs the shopping basket from my hand, tossing a couple of his own items in. "Filthy girl, we're in *public*."

"City girl rolls in to scandalize the cute small town over Christmas. Fun new Hallmark movie, by the sounds of it."

"Meh, I've been scandalizing this town for five years," he says nonchalantly, tossing a bag of ketchup chips in with our strange assortment of supplies. "You sprain *one* kid's wrist outside the corner store, and suddenly you're public enemy number one."

"What?" I laugh, clutching his muscular forearm with my free hand. It feels right. This moment. Him and I leisurely strolling the aisles of the grocery store like a couple, grabbing junk food so we can hole up at home for days on end.

"Long story," he says.

There's a noticeable shift when Lucas sets the basket next to the checkout conveyor. The oxygen's been sucked from the room, everything falling still around us. After finishing a chat with the customer ahead of us—one that was lively and sweeping—the young, bubbly cashier's expression turns sour at the sight of the man beside me.

Maybe she's friends with that other customer, and that's why she was so personable.

I didn't even know the act of purchasing groceries could be awkward, but this is. Painfully so. Not that Lucas seems to mind. He appears just as put out and sour as the woman across the counter.

When he slides his card into the reader, I catch the eye of the cashier, and give her a slight smile, which she doesn't return.

＊＊＊＊＊

"So, what do we think that cashier's story is?" I pull the kitten from my pocket and buckle my seatbelt. "Scorned by a cowboy, definitely. Or was it her little brother whose wrist you sprained?"

Air cuts across his teeth with a quick inhale. "I might've left halfway through our first date."

My heart flip flops. Gripping the belt strapped across my chest, I turn to him.

"*First date?* Did you pick her up during her spare block and go to the corner store to get a slushy? Or go watch a high school football game?"

"I'm already the guy who ditched the pastor's daughter halfway through our date, *and* I accidentally hurt some other kid. Please don't say that shit so loud. You'll make people think I'm a predator."

There's something hot and turbid and clenching in my stomach. For once, I shut up. My palm drags down the kitten's back, a little rougher than I intended. And when I steal a glance over at Lucas, I realize how fucked I am.

I'm jealous.

I'm *jealous?!*

Jealous of him going on a crappy date—so crappy he left halfway through—with a girl who looks like she still has a curfew.

What the fuck is wrong with me?

I lick my suddenly chapped lips and exhale a little louder than I mean to. No doubt it comes off as pouty, but I'm praying he reads it as disgust. A way more understandable reaction.

"It was a *blind* date, for the record." He tosses a hand onto my headrest and twists in his seat to back us out of the parking spot. "My realtor, Margaret, wouldn't stop trying to set me up on dates after I moved to town, so I finally agreed to go. Jenna, the cashier, was *twenty* at the time—in case the FBI are listening in on this conversation. Nothing illegal, but the date was awful."

"So bad she's giving you the death glare in the grocery store."

"I don't know why. I left early because she was obnoxiously hung up on her ex."

"Now she wants you, because she saw us together. Us girls tend to want guys we can't have," I say, unwrapping a piece of gum in hopes it'll stop the tension headache that all this jaw clenching is bound to induce.

His eyes saunter down my body, too slow for somebody who's driving. "Do you want that?"

I gulp. "I mean... yeah."

If I didn't, I wouldn't be setting myself up for heartache by spending all week with him. One night six months ago left me comparing every guy I've met since then to Lucas. How ruined will I be after this?

"Damn. Ruthless to say you want a different guy while I'm *right here*." He slaps the leather truck seat next to his thigh to punctuate the last two words, shaking his head with a funny look.

"Your body might be here, but I don't know where the hell your brain's gone. What are you talking about?"

"You want what you can't have. You can have me. I'm right here, but now you're saying you don't want that."

I laugh awkwardly, assessing the situation to see how to play this. Is he seriously hurt? Or just dicking around? *Fuck*, I can't tell because he's wearing his trademarked cocky look with his arrogant jawline, suckable lips, and enviable eyelashes.

"But I *can't* have you," I practically shout. The chill girl vibes have been compromised. *Fuck.* "I mean... I can for a few days, but we turn into pumpkins or whatever when the clock strikes midnight on Boxing Day."

"Pumpkins?"

"Or snowmen. Cinderella but make it Christmas-y." I flail my hands, clearly losing any semblance of composure. "Anyway, my comment doesn't pertain to you. I want a fictional man from one of my favourite books to sweep me off my feet—*that* is what I meant when I said I want a man I can't have."

Yeah, sure, Eira. I'm mentally rolling my eyes at myself.

"Right. Duh." His fingers drum on the steering wheel. "My comment was stupid. Ignore that."

Ignore his comment? As if.

You can have me. I'm right here. Thanks to those words, I'm going to require a few business days to loosen whatever's cinching around my heart like a corset.

Chapter Eleven

Lucas

It's a two person job to bathe the tiny kitten, despite the fact that it can't weigh more than two pounds. And because I was apparently a total wimp about it biting me earlier, Eira insisted on being the one to hold the cat still while I scrubbed.

"Let me take a turn holding her," I say, looking at the thin scratches covering her hands, then to the pained expression between her brows.

"It's fine," she grits out.

In protest, I set down the bottle of baby shampoo we bought from the grocery store. "Let me. *Please*. You're getting all scratched up."

"Then we'll both get scratched up, and you'll whine about it all night because you didn't want to save her in the first place."

I'm not a sick and twisted cat killer, despite my lapse in judgement before I spoke earlier. It's simply that farms have so many barn cats they actually become a pest, especially when they're feral.

Case in point: the kitten drags a claw across the webbing next to Eira's thumb. She curses under her breath and, rather than letting her call the shots, I simply step in close and grab the cat from her hands.

"Thank you," Eira whispers, taking a nip of bourbon.

Then she gets to work bathing while I grit my teeth and focus on the beautiful woman who's close enough I can feel the sizzle of electricity between our skin. The magnetic pull that's coursed through my veins since the first time I saw her in the bar.

When her hand brushes over mine, there's a split second where I kick myself for not listening to my family and selling this place. If I'd already pulled that trigger, nothing would stop me from moving closer to the city. Maybe not downtown, but I could do the suburbs. I could live less than an hour from her so we could meet for dinner a couple times during the week and take turns spending weekends at her place or mine. We could find out whether this chemistry and connection has staying power.

"What made you decide to become a farrier?" she asks, and I look over to find her studying me with the same intensity she had while drawing in the barn earlier.

"Unlike you, I had a *great* experience with horses as a little kid." I nudge her side. "My family was firmly in the suburbs, but after high school, I moved to Alberta and hung out with a couple guys who rode bulls. Rodeo—especially roughstock, like bull riding—isn't for me, but I met a cool old guy there who offered cash work helping him out with his farrier business. Eventually, that turned into an apprenticeship."

After ensuring the last of the suds rinsed away, she grabs a bath towel and delicately wraps it around the tiny, angry creature. And despite the hissing, Eira places the tiniest kiss right on the kitten's nose.

"I think we should call her Half-Pint."

"Not a bad name," I say, unable to stop smiling at the two of them. I'm not a cat person, but I *am* an Eira Davies person. And for some godforsaken reason, she loves this vicious, two-pound furball. "How 'bout you go get warm and dry by the fire, and I'll grab the cat food?"

Rising to her tiptoes, she places a dainty kiss on my cheek before practically skipping away with her feral bundle of joy.

Armed with wet cat food and a first aid kit, I saunter into the living room a minute later. The small bowl clangs against the tile surrounding the wood stove, and Half-Pint loudly hisses from the cozy bed Eira made her next to the fire.

"*Very intimidating.*" I laugh, cautiously setting the bowl down and taking a giant step back. Because, if I'm being honest, I *am* a little intimidated. I'm not willingly putting my hands near that beast again anytime soon.

"You scared her," Eira scolds. "She's a sweet baby... just gonna take time to warm up."

"I think we should name her Harriet. Or *no*, the most evil of all—*Nancy.* That cat of yours might be the same level of psychopath." Naming her after one of the two most notorious *Little House on the Prairie* characters would suit her better than something as cute and innocent as Half-Pint.

"Half-Pint and Nancy are both misunderstood," Eira states, watching me spread first aid supplies across the coffee table.

I pull an antiseptic wipe and start dabbing at the crooked, crimson scratches on Eira's arm, taking it slow and wincing alongside her every time she inhales sharply through her teeth.

"Nancy locked a girl in the ice house and she almost died. She's disturbed." I swipe antibiotic ointment over the deeper cuts first, kicking myself for not grabbing more in town. I suspect this isn't the last time I'll be taking care of Eira in this way. She's already eyeballing the cat like she wants to scoop it up for a snuggle.

"The amount of Walnut Grove lore you know is astounding." She looks away from the kitten just long enough to raise a brow at me. "Thank you for fixing me up, doc."

"I've got a set of leather gloves out in the truck. *Please* wear them next time you handle that demon spawn."

"We'll be out of your hair soon enough, you old grump." She smiles wistfully, but the thought of her leaving in a few days makes my hands start to shake while I try to wrap a bandage around her forearm. The cat is welcome to leave anytime, but damn would I love to keep Eira clear through to January. Even beyond that, if she let me.

"Want to know a secret of mine?" Bandage secured, I rub my thumb in slow circles over her wrist with enough pressure I feel her heart start to race.

"All of them," she whispers back.

"I have every season of *Little House* on DVD."

Her hair flits around her face with a full-body laugh. "I *knew* it!"

Slapping a hand on my thigh, I start to stand. "You get cozy—maybe try to lure that cat into its box before she finds a way to destroy my house—and I'll go grab 'em."

Already heading toward the cat, which I *know* she's going to scoop up barehanded again, she beams at me. "Bring back the bourbon, too, Charles."

Chapter Twelve

Eira

December 24

"Y our cat howled all night," Lucas grumbles into the pillow next to me.

"She was probably lonely downstairs. I told you we should've brought her in here."

Rolling to his side, he sweeps a large hand over my head and smiles. "I don't love the thought of her looking at me when I'm naked."

"Don't tell me a tiny kitten makes you self-conscious," I say under the sweet dusting of his kisses down my neck.

"Mmm no," he murmurs into my hair. "More fear that she'll remove my dick from my body the first chance she gets. Anyway, enough about your devil cat—"

"No wonder she hisses at you so much. I would, too, if you constantly referred to me as evil."

"Oh, baby, you're evil, all right." He smirks, and I tease him with my scariest hiss. Lucas responds by giving a small nip to my earlobe. "Only a true siren could lure me away from work and into the shower like you did yesterday."

My back arches, hips rolling into him. "In that case, let me beguile you again."

"No time, temptress." The covers pull back, and suddenly he's practically yanking me from the bed with his hand linked in mine. "Merry Christmas Eve, Doodlebug. We have a lot to do in order to have your no-pants holiday tomorrow."

Being in bed with him all day would easily put this Christmas in my top three. Just after that Christmas when Dad's office Christmas party Santa—who smelled like cigarettes and cheddar cheese—gave me a hundred dollar bill, but probably before the year Holly and I pub-crawled on Christmas Eve.

At this exact moment, I care very little about having a movie-like holiday, but I roll out of bed and drag a hand down my face with a groan. Then pad behind him to the bathroom.

"What exactly do you have on this list?" I ask, reaching for sunscreen and methodically swiping it over my face.

He holds up a finger until he's done brushing his teeth then licks his lips and smiles at me. "First things first, we need a real tree."

* * * * *

Knowing my fear of horses, Lucas suggested we take his truck. But not before making a sassy comment about a horseback ride up the mountain being more romantic. Now snuggled up in his truck's bench seat, I couldn't disagree more. My palm rubs the length of his thigh, my head rests on his shoulder, and he periodically presses his lips to my hairline. Warm, cozy, and stealing quick kisses every chance we get, I can't think of a better way to find the perfect tree.

"How about that one?" I point to the left hand side, sitting straighter with excitement.

Lucas slows the truck to a crawl. "Not gonna work, baby. Look at the base—you got two trees tangled up in each other there instead of one."

"Mmm, sounds romantic." I walk my fingers up to his chest, slipping under the collar. "Also sounds a lot like us last night."

"God, I can't wait to lay you down under the Christmas tree and watch the lights dance on your naked body."

My core tightens, and I blink up at him, searching his face and hoping I'll somehow find the words to say written in the small creases around his eyes or the peppered stubble on his jawline.

"Get back to tree hunting, Doodlebug. You're slacking on the job."

Doubling down on the intensity of my gaze, I meet his deep blue eyes. "Petition to make my new job staring at you."

"You're hired. Although I think you'll discover how boring I am and decide to quit."

"I'm an artist—people watching is *never* boring."

The truck careens through a large pothole, and I squeeze my hands around his sculpted bicep for stability. Somehow both hands barely fit, something I spend a moment measuring so I can take it home with me.

The feel of my hands on his smooth skin, the drum of his heart when I lay my head on his chest in bed, the taste of his lips on mine—all that and so many more pieces of Lucas I can't put onto paper as easily as I can the roped veins in his forearms and the freckles on his shoulders.

Glancing out the window, I spot a tree that looks *exactly* like one you'd see in a Hallmark Christmas movie. I swear there's even a beam of sunshine streaming through the clouds in that singular spot.

"Stop!" I point excitedly. "That's the one."

The truck grinds to a halt on the icy back road, and Lucas follows my sightline with a smile. "That's the one. Let's go cut it down."

Once again wearing Lucas's clothes, I hold one hand on the waist of my pants and trudge through the deep snow behind him, mindful my feet don't slide right out of the much-too-large winter boots. I feel ridiculous, but he looks at me over his shoulder and holds out a hand with enchantment gleaming in his eyes.

The tree's farther from the road than I expected, and I'm slightly out of breath when we reach it. But excitement sparks under my skin when I circle the massive fir, envisioning how we'll decorate it with lights, and garland, and...

"Oh." Every ounce of Christmas joy hardens and crumbles away like a burnt sugar cookie. "It's flat on this side. It looked perfect from the truck…"

Lucas shushes me, shaking snow from the branches, clearly disregarding the fact that I just told him this tree isn't any good.

"Doodlebug, this isn't a tree farm, so whichever one we pick is bound to have some imperfections. But the best trees have character." He sweeps a foot along the ground, then squats down with his saw in hand. "Besides, we wouldn't be here if you hadn't drawn a picture of me with a super flat ass. I think you have a thing for flat backsides."

I laugh, scooping a snowball in my gloved hands and hitting him in the back with it.

"Didn't anybody ever tell you not to get in a fight with a man carrying a saw?" He twists to look at me, slowly straightening back up. There's something menacing and fiery in his eye. Something that tells me to run.

With my first lumbering steps, he's lunging in my direction. The saw sinks out of sight in the deep snow, and I nervously laugh while running in the most awkward, inelegant way across the open field.

Lucas's arm snags around my waist, pulling me to him, and together we topple—a knee-deep snow drift cushioning our fall. Flakes cling to his coat and hair and eyelashes, and he claims me with a kiss. We fight each other for oxygen, with roaming hands and melting snow soaking through our clothes. We're passionate and impatient, taking everything we can until my heart feels as if it might burst from my chest.

"You're so fucking beautiful." His lips ghost over mine. "Let's go get your perfect tree."

Swallowing hard, I kiss him one last time before letting him pull me to my feet. He meticulously brushes the snow from my clothing, though it's too late; I'm cold and soaked to the bone, while also the happiest I've ever been.

✳ ✳ ✳ ✳ ✳

I unwrap the towel from around my chest and pull a pair of leggings over my red-tinted legs. Skipping the bra, I slip into a waffle-knit long sleeve. Lucas demanded I take a hot bath while he ran down to the barn to check on the horses, and I'm never one to turn down a nice soak. But I only stayed in the sudsy water long enough to defrost, wanting the alone time to finish my drawing of Lucas in the stables.

Half-Pint meows a greeting when I enter the living room.

"Hi, little one." I toss the drawing pad and pencils onto the couch, then peel open a bag of cat treats. Nodding toward the tree propped up in the corner, I add, "If I give you these treats, you have to promise not to ruin the Christmas tree."

She hisses, and I choose to believe that means she agrees.

I sink into the couch, reaching to scoop up Half-Pint—only receiving one minor scratch this time. She settles easily onto the cushion next to me for a liver treat-induced slumber, and I lose myself in Lucas again. His posture and taut muscles and intense focus as he worked. Never have I dreamt of being a horse-hoof before today, but I'd be okay having him lay me over his thick thigh like that.

Shortly after I've completed the finishing touches, the front door swings open, bringing a rush of frigid air alongside a hot-as-sin mountain man.

I meet him in the foyer, stretching to kiss him softly while brushing the snow from his shoulders and unzipping his coat. Stripping the layers and letting them fall in a damp heap on the floor with one hand, I stroke the coarse stubble on his jaw with the other.

"Let's go decorate that tree before I get too caught up in carrying you off to bed." He squeezes my ass. "Santa won't come if we don't have a tree set up."

My head tips back to let him drag his tongue over my pulse point. "There's no way he's leaving us anything but coal anyway. You're way too naughty."

Lucas chuckles. "You're one to talk, snow angel."

Arm around my waist, he urges me back into the living room and slides a large tote in my direction. Popping the lid off, I find an assortment of decorations and lights. It seems a lot of them are childhood ornaments, including some hand-made pieces labelled with a child's illegible printing—likely Lucas's.

"These are incredible." I pull out a popsicle stick picture frame with a photo of him from the first grade. Then a tiny SpongeBob SquarePants wearing a Santa hat.

"Yeah, my mom bought something to represent each of us to hang on the tree every year. And then gifted us our own boxes of ornaments when my sisters and I moved out." After ensuring the tree's snug in its stand, he takes a step back to admire it.

Not wanting to intrude on what I imagine is a special part of his Christmas tradition—the unboxing and placing of thir-ty-two years' worth of ornaments—I focus on making sure the red and green lights sit perfectly on the branches. I wince at the sting of needles pricking my skin, suddenly feeling a tiny bit thankful for growing up with a fake, non-stabby tree. But every inhale brings a forest scent, and the crackling fire ambience is so Hallmark it fills my chest with dancing sugarplum fairies.

"There's one here for you, Doodlebug." His voice catches me off-guard, and I peek around from the back of the tree to look at him.

"For... me?"

"Obviously, I didn't know you were going to be here early enough for me to get you a proper ornament, so I cut a round from the bottom of the tree." He blushes, holding up a perfect wood circle, a hole drilled through it for a piece of string. Our names and the year written in sharpie, in a much more legible font than the preschool ornament I saw earlier.

"Lucas, stop. That's the best gift anyone has ever given me." My arms loop around his neck, and the ornament bounces over my back with his tight embrace.

It's official, a McKinney Ranch Christmas is better than any movie.

"Wow, you've had some shitty gifts."

My laughter is guttural, emotion thick and uncomfortable in my throat. I blink away the burning under my eyelids and press the side of my head to his firm chest.

"Lots of good gifts. None as thoughtful, though." I clutch the piece of wood to my chest, scanning the tree for a suitable branch. "Where should we put it?"

"Left a vacant spot front and centre. As it deserves."

The ornament dangles from the branch, spinning clockwise then counterclockwise, catching the light with every turn.

"What's next on the list of things you *always* do on the ranch during Christmas?" I doubted him the second he said my Christmas vision was his norm—given he's a bachelor who couldn't be bothered to spend the holiday with his loving family—but it hasn't gone unnoticed, or unloved, how much effort he's making. I ease back into his embrace, his fingertips catching my chin and forcing my gaze to meet his.

"Baked goods. Lots of it. I bought out everything the bakery had left yesterday, so we can really make good use of your no-pants holiday style."

I smile against his lips. "No pants and desserts are my love language."

Chapter Thirteen

Lucas

S nagging our bourbon glasses and a tin of cookies I bought from the bakery, I traipse into the living room and stop to toss a couple pieces of wood into the stove before sitting next to her. She's holding the cat like a human infant, tree lights flickering over them in a random pattern. Damn, if only I was an artist. She looks like a fucking painting.

Half-Pint stretches her front legs, eyes pleading with me not to kick her out of her comfortable spot.

"Look as cute as you want. I'm still convinced you're evil." I move to boop the cat's nose, and she swats at me. "Case in point."

"Oh, shush." Eira's fingers rap over my forearm, but she tilts until her head's resting on my chest. I inhale her sweet scent, looking over at the first Christmas tree I've had in this house.

When I saw a photo of the rundown farmhouse in a small town I'd never stepped foot in, I knew in my bones it was meant to be mine. Not a reservation or second thought. It had been listed the same day as my accident two years prior.

My head screamed coincidence; my heart whispered fate.

And that same murmuring filled my chest and exploded through the synapses in my brain when, six months ago, Eira and I spent a night laughing, sharing secrets, and filling the air between us with the buzz of sexual tension. When I lay awake in bed that night, I could've stayed in that moment forever.

My finger traced her hairline, brushing a soft lock of dark hair away from her temple. I drew the shell of her ear, and the curve of her creamy cheek, swallowing hard when I switched to running the back of my knuckles over her face.

Her dark eyelashes fluttered, making my heart race and hand still. No doubt it would be awkward if she caught me delicately touching her as she slept, doing my best to soak in every second with her.

When her breathing steadied, I smoothed my hardened palm over her hair. And I risked a kiss, because it was impossible not to with that stunning woman curled up in my arms.

The moment my lips touched her forehead, she mumbled something that sounded a lot like my name, nuzzling in even closer.

Could've been my brain playing tricks on me. Honestly? Probably was. But even the tiniest chance that she was dreaming about me was enough to fill my chest with the wrenching pain of regret.

Just one night. That's all she wanted, and all I thought I could offer. But fuck *would I have loved that one night to last a lifetime.*

Eira breaks the silence with a sweet kiss on the back of my hand. "Whatcha thinking about?"

My eyebrows furrow while I try to come up with something that won't put her in a weird place when we both know she has to go home in a couple days. "What made you decide to illustrate?"

She glances over at me with a bourbon-glazed smile. "I don't even think I have an answer, because I can't remember a time when I wasn't drawing. But I didn't know how to make money at it, so it stayed a hobby until a little over a year ago when my friend asked me to draw a book cover design for her. It's been snowballing since then. I'm so tired of being treated like crap at my corporate job—the dream is to have enough steady commission work to quit one day."

"So, you're telling me that you'll draw me naked if I pay you to?" My drink trickles down my throat, and I watch her intently over the rim of my glass. There's a new rouging of her cheeks and chest—based on my experience, it continues under her clothes.

"Well... in that case, it's a commission. And I can't turn down a commission."

"Great. How much?"

The wallet tucked into my coat pocket by the front door is probably sobbing. The thought of spending money on anything that isn't a necessity sends my stomach roiling, especially after I blew over a hundred dollars on random food and supplies to give her the perfect Christmas. Not to mention, I texted the therapeutic riding facility's stable manager after convincing Eira to come with me yesterday, to let her know I could only shoe half the number of horses we'd agreed upon. I'll get to them next week, working a couple extra-long days to make up the lost wages.

But even if I can't recoup the money I lost yesterday, I don't care. It's worth it. I'd bet the farm on her.

"Considering you bought all these incredible desserts"—she flourishes a Nanaimo bar through the air—"and you're giving me a warm bed to sleep in, I think I can cut you a deal."

* * * * *

Tossing back two ounces of bourbon, I wish I'd grabbed something higher proof. I know all of this was my idea, but that doesn't mean I'm immune to nervous jitters.

The bedside lamp flickers slightly before fully illuminating the small space, and Eira belly flops onto the bed with a warm laugh. Markers and notepad spread across the deep green comforter, she smiles up at me.

"Socks."

"Who starts with socks?" I squint at her.

"Who ends with socks?" She rests her chin in her hands, feet kicking behind her. "Anyway, who's in charge here?"

Rolling my eyes, I bend and pull off my socks, then chuck them in the hamper next to my dresser.

Eira whistles a catcall. "Damn, boy."

Laughing, I say, "If you have a foot fetish, I am *not* your man."

She shifts a little, picking up a pencil and drawing something near the top of the page that I can't quite make out. It better be my head and not the start of a giant foot picture.

"Not a foot girl, but I was a big fan of the forearm flex when you gave the left sock an extra firm tug. Speaking of which, lose the shirt," she says without looking up from the graceful glide of pencil on paper.

The hem catches on my fingers, and I tug upward slowly, waiting for the moment her eyes flutter to look at me through her thick lashes. I give her a wink before pulling the fabric overhead.

A heavy rise and fall of her chest makes my cock pulse under my jeans. She studies my bare upper body in the shallow light, crinkling her nose as she slowly drags pencil over paper. The only sounds in the room are my heartbeat and the gentle scratch of lead in her notebook.

"Pants," she says the word with the exasperation of somebody running a marathon.

"Shouldn't belt be its own category?" I grip the buckle, staring her down.

The snap as I unbuckle it makes her bite down on her lower lip. The leather glides through the loops on my jeans. Eira's eyes widen, pupils blown out with lust, as I loop it between my hands and tug until the leather slaps together. The sound reverberates through the room, and even I have goosebumps on the back of my neck. Then I let the entire thing fall to the wooden floor with a resounding thunk.

Her gaze flits to the belt then back to me. "You were right. That *definitely* deserves to be its own category."

"Now pants?" I can't help the love-drunk smile, or the cadence of my heartbeat, slamming into every rib and spreading out through my limbs. I want to drop the pants and go to her, tell her to forget about the drawing idea, and feel the warmth of her words on my skin.

With a heady tone, she says, "Now pants."

Drawing in a long breath then releasing it slowly, I let the denim slide down my legs. The last time I felt self-conscious was as a middle schooler in the locker room after gym class. A woman seeing me naked hasn't affected me. But something about this—the slow strip, the scratchy sound of Eira drawing in a frenzy, the warm-toned light bulb, and the slight nip in the air—is making my lungs constrict painfully.

God. I need a way to make me look hot and cool for her.

Crossing my arms over my chest, I lean against the dresser. *But not like I'm trying too hard.*

Uncrossing my arms, I lick my lips and watch her draw. She hasn't even looked up at me since I lost the pants, and her hand's moving around the paper in a frenzy.

"Boxers."

The snap of elastic under my fingers makes her head careen upward, and I'm met with hungry eyes and an inspired twitch at the corner of her mouth. The pencil eraser taps on the notepad, a metronome in the otherwise silent room.

I clear my throat, stopping with my fingers pinching the waistband. "I feel like we should be playing some Ginuwine."

"Hrm. Don't move a muscle."

Tucking the pencil between her teeth, Eira lifts to her hands and knees. And in a move that makes my breath catch in my throat, she crawls across the bed.

If she's not doing that naked later tonight, I might just tear her clothes from her body and make her. She can be bossy? Well, so can I.

Sitting on the edge of my bed, she looks over at me with a sly smile, fingers tapping on her phone screen.

"Better?" With a wink, Eira slowly increases the volume, then sinks back into the small indent her body created in the bedding.

"I take back what I said. Now this just feels slutty."

With a laugh that slides over my body like silky lotion, she turns off the song. "All right, no more lollygagging. Boxers. Off."

"Yes, ma'am."

They slip down to join the jeans pooled around my ankles. With a quick side step, I'm fully exposed, and my hands naturally fall in front of my dick. Or they try to, but it's rock hard and bobbing in front of me, every slow lick of Eira's lips making it twitch.

And she's just *staring.*

I can't tell if she's assessing me or trying to commit it all to memory. The glances at her paper become less frequent, and the slow rake of her eyes over my body take up most of her time.

"This is gonna take a while—might be better for you if you sit." She points her nose toward the armchair in the corner.

Eira catcalls me again the instant I turn to follow her direction.

"You were right. Your ass *is* better out of pants," she says when I give her a look. "And your cock is really pretty. Has anybody told you that before?"

Fuck. That smile of hers has my anxieties collapsing like a house of cards.

"No," I say through a laugh, sinking into the thick cushion. "Nobody has ever complimented my dick before."

"Well, good. I'm glad I'm the first."

For an indeterminate amount of time, she draws quietly and I sit naked, cock at full attention, watching her work. Coming closer and closer to leaping from this chair with every tiny poke of her tongue, every slow sip of bourbon she takes while she considers something, and every fleeting glance my way. My nails sink into the armrests, willing my body to follow her rules and stay still.

I need something to break the tension

It's both the most frustrating and seductive thing I've ever experienced.

"Done," she says with a gasp, as if the drawing comes as a surprise to her. "*Damn.*"

"That bad, huh?" I chuckle. "Thinking you should stick to fictional character porn, or what?"

"Thinking about how all the art I made after our night at the hotel really proves how shit my memory is."

I choke on my own spit for a moment, and she stalks toward me with our shared glass of bourbon. She lets me take a sip to ease the tickle in my throat, then takes a slow gulp herself.

She's been thinking about me that *much?*

"When do I get to see all this art of yours?"

"The others are for me, but I'll let you see this one." With a smirk, she holds up tonight's masterpiece. And it really is a fucking masterpiece. How she was able to sketch every detail, right down to the small birthmark on my thigh, is beyond me.

"Holy shit." I squint to get a better look. "How the hell aren't you a famous artist already?"

A sad sigh slips from between kissable lips. "That's the dream. Well, not fame, necessarily. But I'd love to be able to say I'm a full-time artist."

"You will *definitely* do that someday soon." I shake my head in disbelief. "And you just sketched that in... half an hour, or so? *Damn.*"

Tucking a piece of short, dark hair behind her ear, she scrunches her nose. "Thank you."

"So, what did you do with all the pictures you drew of me?"

"Built a shrine, obviously."

"Good. Bet that deters any man who comes into your apartment."

Just the thought of that has a low growl threatening to rumble in my chest. Not that I own her. But fuck, would I like to.

"Only fictional men allowed in my apartment. No, I just keep them inside my bedside table..." Her sentence trails off, and I'm desperate to know what else is on her mind.

"And? Sounded like you had something to add. What do you do with the pictures, Eira? Do you look at them?" My hand falls to my cock instinctively, and I give it one slow tug.

"Yes."

"Do you look at them with a purpose, or do you just check to make sure nobody has stolen them?"

"It depends." She looks down at the drawing held tight in her hands. "It uh, it depends...on what I feel like."

Say. It.

Admit that I haven't been the only one feeling this sense of yearning for months.

"Sometimes it can be a little more...*useful* to help me get in the mood. But after I draw them... "

"What then?" My words are strained with wanton desperation.

Her cheeks are ruddy, eyes glimmering. "Then I pretend it's you touching me. It's you making me come."

"Show me." Only it comes out so much weaker—groveling and pathetic—than it sounded in my head.

The jump of my cock grabs her startled attention when she takes a step toward me.

"Should I?" she asks hesitantly.

"God, yes."

A huff of pleased air blows from her nose, and she rocks on her heels, taking a few small steps back. Her shirt slips overhead in one smooth motion, and I'm thankful we stopped the music, because I can hear the rasp in every shallow breath she takes.

"Shirt," she says, letting it fall from her fingertips.

Hooking a thumb under the button, she pops open her pants and shimmies then down her legs. "Pants."

"Come here. I take the panties off," I growl.

My hands need her hips, and they have no trouble slipping into the small dips in her curves to position her between my legs.

Her mouth opens, nothing but a breathless moan coming out as my fingers tease her panties aside and slide inside her. Nothing but seeing me naked—*drawing me naked*—has her slick and needy. Ready to put this creative anatomy lesson to good use.

"I bet you didn't know I'm a bit of a painter myself, baby."

She gulps, eyebrows narrowing, then relaxing as my fingers drive deeper. "Oh?"

I withdraw from her pussy, bringing my drenched fingers to trace her pout, and her knees quiver. "I plan on painting this gorgeous body with my cum repeatedly tonight. Fuck, you'll look so good like that."

Her tongue moves over her glistening lips in one languid stroke.

"But first I need to see what you do to yourself when you imagine me."

A gentle push on her hips has her stumbling back toward the bed, her panties slowly falling down her legs with every step. Her ass hasn't even hit the comforter before she's running a finger up her slit.

"That's it, baby."

Her eyes don't leave mine until I grab hold of my dick, and the lust-filled gaze turns intimidating. "*No.* I had to stare at your body for half an hour without touching myself, you can watch."

"I wasn't fucking my hand while you watched, though," I argue. Not that there's any sense in arguing. I'm nothing but pathetic when it comes to her.

I lean back, grabbing hold of the armrests with a grip that implies I'm about to be blasted off into outer space. Honestly? I might be.

Eira glides her fingers inside with a guttural moan that raises the hair at the back of my neck. The throb of desire between my legs has me shifting in place, fighting the urge to help it along.

"You're so fucking beautiful," I mutter as electricity fizzes through my balls.

Finding her clit, she tosses her head back and shakes out her hair while her free hand wraps around a blanket edge. My chest heaves. Head floating through a haze as all the blood in my body races to my groin.

Every whimper ruins me.

My cock's so hard it's painful, and I only grip the chair tighter, sinking deeper into the cushion. Letting my dick cut through the crisp air, thick strands of precum creating a webbing between the head and my bare stomach.

My name leaves her mouth in a wail, like she's all alone in her apartment in the city, turned on and lost in her imagination after drawing my naked body. It does me in.

Without even touching my dick. Without looking at it. Despite her being halfway across the room. Despite her fingers being lost in her pussy, when it should be mine.

I come fucking *undone*.

Balls tight and hot, I hold my breath and focus on Eira's perfectly pink, soaking wet pussy. The air's thick with her scent, and my view of her slowly rubbing her clit becomes dotted as an orgasm builds.

My cock jolts with a mind of its own, twitching and writhing and shooting warm cum onto my stomach. Teeth gritted, I slam a fist down on top of the armrest and shut my eyes to feel the host of emotions in my veins. Embarrassment. Lust. Shock.

The room's silent save for my thrumming pulse.

Catching my breath, I jolt at the sensation of skin on mine. Eira's soft hands skim my bare thighs, then knead the tender muscles, slowly spreading my knees wide. Her bottom lip drags over skin I'm not sure anyone's ever touched before, making it quiver.

"Baby, you're fucking stunning and I—" The explanation floats away in a Viking funeral when the wet, warmth of her tongue greedily laps up the cum running down my shaft. Suddenly I'm engulfed in flames, hips bucking upward. "*Fuuuck.*"

She murmurs my name at the same time the tip of my cock slides between her rose-hued lips. She pulls me in deep, creating suction over the tip that vetoes any need for a refractory period.

"The only thing better than the way it feels when my cock's in your mouth is the way it looks." I push upward until her throat tightens around me with a gag. "That's my pretty girl."

She pulls away, saliva threaded between her lips and the tip of my cock, with glassy eyes and mascara smudged on her creamy skin. After a quick swirl of her tongue around the reddened crown, she sinks her warm mouth back down, bottoming out with a moan.

"I need your pussy around my cock, baby. Right fucking now." I grunt, teeth sinking into the flesh on the back of my hand.

Hollowing her cheeks, Eira pulls a moan from deep in my chest. The quick release of suction snaps something inside me, and I grab a rough hold of her to walk us to bed. She falls backward, hair splayed across the mussed up comforter, and I sling her legs over my shoulders to drive into her pussy in one brutish thrust.

"Oh my God," she cries out, fingers desperately seeking purchase on the bed—needing something to keep her from floating out of her body the way I clung helplessly to the armchair.

Entirely feral, and taking everything like this is the last time, I fuck her so hard I'm sure she'll be sore tomorrow. And that knowledge only encourages me to go harder. I want the feel of my cock branded into the walls of her cunt, something that will remind her of me every time she touches herself after she goes home.

My balls sting with every slap against her ass. Maybe I want that permanent reminder for myself, too. Not that I'm at risk of forgetting her.

"It's so deep." Her nails bite into my forearms.

"You're going to take every last fucking inch," I growl. "This pussy's mine. Don't fucking forget that."

Her eyes widen, nostrils flaring.

"*Mine*, Eira."

I'm fucking losing it.

Whether it's the post-nut clarity or the way I'm already on the verge of coming again mere minutes later. Or maybe I'm losing my mind because it's Christmas Eve, and I'm balls deep inside a woman I didn't expect to care so much about.

My brain knows this comes to an end in a couple days; my heart refuses to not to be in it for the long haul. And I can't fucking stand that.

Chapter Fourteen

Eira

Though the way his fingers strum over my clit is delicate, nothing in the aggressive thrusts or deep-etched scowl on his face is. His skin slaps into mine each time I'm filled to the hilt—so deep it borders on painful.

My back lifts off the bed with the wave of an impending orgasm, heat swirling in my core, edged by the angry grunts and groans that slip out from between his tight lips. Like pain and pleasure are waging war inside him.

My eyelids slam shut, and my ankles tighten around his neck.

So close.

So close.

"Open your fucking eyes," Lucas barks. "Open them and look at me."

This doesn't feel like the time to argue, so I gaze up at him, wide-eyed as his tight, hurried circles on my clit make my walls clench around him, and we're both staving off the inevitable.

"Please," I beg quietly. "I-I'm gonna..."

"Come," he orders, somehow finding a way to make every thrust even more powerful.

Legs shaking, pulse racing, core tightening, an orgasm overwhelms me. And his eyes soften a little when he pulls out to paint the apex of my thighs in thick, white cum.

The muscles in his jaw tense, and a low rumble claws its way up from his chest as he reaches between us. His index finger drags through the substance glistening on my pale skin, tracing a well-defined L. Then another letter next to it.

LM

With attention to detail, he cleans up the tail end of the M, as if there was ever any doubt what he was asserting.

"Lucas," I barely squeak out, staring at where his finger is still hovering just above my skin. Above where he laid claim by signing his initials like an artist branding a completed work.

In the next moment, the only movement is the staggered rise and fall of our chests. Then he removes my ankles from his muscular shoulders and steps backward.

"I'll go get you a washcloth." His voice is gruff, and the bunching between his eyebrows still evident.

What the hell changed in the last five minutes?

He was flirty and funny and himself while I sketched. Feeling safe, I showed him what I drew. He insisted I touch myself so he could watch, and he came without even touching his cock. And when I sucked the saltiness off his warm skin, he lovingly sifted a hand through my hair.

But the moment he thrust into me, something snapped. I got a fascinating glimpse of the gruff, angry, closed-off version of Lucas people warned me about. I'm not against rough sex, the sting of damp skin colliding repeatedly, the sweat running past his temple from the aggressive thrusting, or the angry dirty talk. I know Lucas, though—enough to know that wasn't fun for him.

"Thank you." I extend a hand to take the damp towel when he saunters back into the room.

With a sudden tenderness, Lucas sinks down onto the mattress next to me and quietly says, "Let me do it."

A shiver skates up my spine when the warm cloth presses to my lower stomach. Without a word, he cleans me, the tiniest flicker of a lost smile catching my eye when I whimper at the feel of his touch floating over my clit.

As silently as he came in, he leaves. I use that opportunity to check on the kitten while he showers, and hopefully clears whatever's on his mind. He's still in the shower when I open the bathroom door to brush my teeth.

In spite of the tension, I curl my fingers around the shower door handle. An hour ago, I would've slipped in after him without question, kissing him deeply and maybe suggesting we go for round two. But now I don't know what's going on.

What if he's as sullen and closed off as people say, and now that he's gotten what he wants, he's driving me away?

My eyes dart to the door, debating if I should sneak away and go back to the cabin. Except I really don't want to leave tonight. Part of me doesn't want to leave, period.

I sat with thoughts of staying for the entire drive back to the ranch after the day at the stables and a drive past the elementary school to see the snowmen Lucas loves. I found myself inadvertently scanning store windows in town for *Help Wanted* signs, as if I could pack it all up and move to Fox Ridge. Hell, I'd even settle for a snowstorm that keeps me here until the new year.

But now...

"Come in here, Doodlebug."

Releasing a pent-up breath, I slip into the steamy box, and his hands instantly find their way to my hips. In spite of the unanswered questions and ache in my chest over his potential answers, I lap up his touch.

Once I'm fully enveloped in his arms, my heartbeat becomes indistinguishable from his, and Lucas stops the Earth from spinning altogether with a ravaging kiss. Wet hands grabbing either side of my face, stealing my breath with the firm stroke of his tongue on mine, and shutting up every anxious thought in my brain.

I still have to leave after Christmas. But right now, I'm his.

"Are you okay?" he asks quietly.

"That was unexpectedly rough, but I'm fine." I tuck into the space under his jaw. "Are you?"

"I got a little lost in my head."

"Happens to the best of us."

"And then I just got angry—not at you. Angry with myself for... feeling." A half laugh slips out of him. "Wow, hearing that thought out loud... *yikes.* If you're sore at all, I'll draw you a bath while I feed you Christmas cookies and wash your hair to make up for it."

"In that case..." I groan dramatically, keeling over in mock pain. "Make sure you condition it, too. And while you do all that, you can tell me about this big, elusive, scary feeling."

He sighs, and that alone tells me how hard he's grappling with something. "Fate is so fucking cruel to only give me a small taste of what having you is like. To show me what I can't have... It's infuriating."

My lips roll together, and I fidget with a lock of wet hair. There are so many things I could say, but shouldn't. So many things I should say but can't.

What a fucking mess we've created.

"And now you're completely freaked out, probably thinking I'll lock you in this house to keep you forever or something."

I shrug casually. "I get it. If I thought talking with you all night at the bar—and then your hotel room—was the best night I'd ever had, this has been..."

No words.

"Yeah..."

No words from him, either.

"Yeah," I concur.

One more day together, and regardless of our feelings, this conversation doesn't warrant more than a *yeah*. I have a job and a life in the city. He has a job and a life here. Does it suck? A little.

Okay...a lot.

✶✶✶✶✶

"Merry Christmas," Lucas whispers in my ear before I've fully awoken. For a moment, I let him think I'm still asleep, revelling in his soft breath against my shoulder and the feather-light touch of his fingertips stroking my hair.

And I do my best not to dwell on the what ifs. That was the promise we made while he washed my hair—in the shower, not bath, because I was rushing to curl up next to him under the covers. We agreed that December twenty-sixth was something we'd face no earlier than 11:59 p.m. on Christmas day.

When I peel open my eyes, sunlight's streaming in through his bedroom window, blanketing our bodies in a pink-hued morning glow. And Lucas is looking at me with a smile that rivals the sunshine. Like a small child on Christmas morning, he's practically bouncing in place, and my heart rate innately speeds up to match his.

"Morning," I rasp, half-closing my eyes until they adjust to the wild world around me. "What time is—"

"I made you breakfast," he blurts out. "Also coffee with some kind of candy cane creamer from the grocery store, which, given the expiry date is *seven* months from now, is definitely not a real dairy product."

"I think I found the type of Christmas person who scares me even more than the marathon runners." I rub the sleepies from my eyes and slowly sit up, adjusting the fit of his T-shirt over my shoulders. After working through a loud and long yawn, I say, "The whole point of Christmas is to relax, which includes staying in bed as late as you want."

"If that's not the sign of an only child, I don't know what is." With a rather convincing pouty look, he manages to lure me from the warmth of his bed. And I'm begrudgingly dragging my bare feet across his wooden floorboards as he continues to yammer on. "In my house, the presents would've all been stolen, with the exception of my new underwear and socks, and breakfast demolished by this time in the morning."

"But there are no presents under this tree, and the only one who might steal our food is Half-Pint."

He holds my hands down the stairs, probably assuming I'm too sleep-deprived to function. A valid assumption, given we were up until well past two a.m. alternating between talking about past holiday memories and having slow, luxurious sex to make up for earlier.

"She already had her own piece of French toast, so she better not."

Something flutters in my chest. "You made her Christmas breakfast?"

"No." He glances over his shoulder at me as we walk into the kitchen, which is heavily scented with cinnamon and nutmeg and sugar and wood fire. And Half-Pint is sitting next to a tea saucer on the floor, staring us down as she licks her tiny lips.

"I didn't make her breakfast"—Lucas crouches to pick up the saucer, fast enough that Half-Pint's incoming open paw barely misses his forearm—"I was simply making a sacrifice to the demon spawn. Something to keep her from murdering me in my sleep. Cats do that, you know."

I hide a breathy laugh behind my fist, sinking down into a chair at the table. He really wasn't kidding about having a full breakfast prepared. Bacon, sausage, eggs, French toast, fresh fruit, and a steaming mug of coffee.

"Wow... What time did you get up to do all this?" I bend to pet Half-Pint, who's weaving around my legs, rubbing her head over my ankles.

"Six a.m." He drops a couple pieces of bacon onto my plate then his own.

"What the fuck?" My jaw drops at the thought of this man getting no more than three hours of sleep before making me a gourmet meal. "Lucas, I seriously did not need all of this."

"You're trusting me to give you a movie-worthy experience on your favourite no-pants holiday. A massive feast to start off sounds like a good way to make that happen."

"Speaking of which, why are *you* wearing pants?" I gesture to his jeans—of all the pants, *jeans?*

"Because you look fucking hot in nothing but my T-shirt. It's taking everything in me not to slip my hands underneath, grab hold of your hips, and pull you into my lap." He bites his lip, blowing out an exasperated exhale. It really is hard on him. "On the other hand, I would look like a knock-off Winnie the Pooh."

I reach for my coffee. "That doesn't sound bad at all."

"Oh, believe me. I took a look in the mirror this morning." He pulls a disgusted face. "I'll lose the pants when the moment calls for it—not a second sooner. How's breakfast?"

"This is definitely better than the cookies and creme breakfast cereal I brought along with me to eat today. Honestly, I think this might be a five-star stay, Mr. McKinney."

I can't help but notice his attempt at discretion as he slips a tiny piece of bacon underneath the table.

"Who knew I'd have such a hardass for a first guest. If you're waffling between this being worth five stars or not, I'd hate to see what you rate other places."

I shake my fork pointedly at him. "Waffles. *That's it.* That would definitely bump it to five stars. Fuck, I love a continental breakfast with one of those make-your-own-waffle machines."

I chew the piece of French toast that's been parading through the air for the past thirty seconds.

"The thing is, after what you did to my soup pot, I'm a little uneasy about the idea of you and a waffle maker."

"The waffle is done so fast, there's no time for me to get too involved in drawing monster smut. That truly is my downfall. I'm just a girl, and I lose my head a bit when orcs are involved." My cheeks light on fire, and I awkwardly brush a strand of nothing away from my face.

Expectedly, Lucas laughs. But not in the way guys have laughed about my passion when I tell them on dates—not that I've ever mentioned *orcs* on dates. Usually, the casual conversation about illustrating book covers for romance novels is enough for them to deem it unworthy of dedicating so much time to.

Fuck those guys.

"Once again asking to see your artwork." Lucas takes a slow sip of coffee. "Given what I've seen so far, you might put me on to monster porn somehow."

"Okay..." Biting back a smile, I do my best to hide the nerves with a curt nod. "After breakfast I can show you some things I've worked on."

"Good girl," he says in a low growl, knowing *exactly* what the hell he's doing.

Fuck, if he didn't hold me to my promise. In fact, the moment we finished cleaning up the kitchen, he grabbed me by the hem of my—er, *his*—shirt and pressed a quick kiss to my forehead before saying he was ready to be enlightened by monster dicks.

No pressure.

Settling in next to the Christmas tree, I pull Half-Pint into my lap, much to Lucas's fake chagrin. My iPad powers up, and I give him one last cursory glance, waiting for any hint that this is going to send him running for the hills.

Then I open my drawing app, tap on a recent commission, and shut my eyes while it loads.

"Wait, this is really cool." He pulls the tablet from my hands, disbelief evident in the parting of his lips and the slow shake of his head. "I said it before, and I'm gonna keep saying it until I find some rich motherfucker who has some serious pull in the art scene and I force him to hear me out even though I'm a farrier with no clue about art—you should be fucking famous."

Burying my face in my hands, I mutter a thank you.

"Can I look at some others?"

Looking up at him with a jumble of gut-wrenching fear and an overwhelming desire to kiss him, I nibble my thumbnail. "Um...yeah, sure. Some are a little more, uh, *explicit* than others."

Time drags during his intensive study of each illustration. Anxiety creeps into the marrow of my bones, travels through my veins, and not even the wonderful compliments he gives does anything to stop it.

That is, until he gasps. "Hold on...is this... Oh, you fucking minx, you. Is this us, Eira?"

The tablet spins and I'm face-to-face with a *graphic* visual of us beside a Christmas tree—something I made after meeting with Holly for coffee on the day she asked if I'd be willing to spend Christmas here. It was simply a way of creating the daydream stuck on a loop in my head. And *obviously*, I didn't imagine Lucas would ever see it. Nobody ever gets to see the work-in-progresses I keep saved on this device.

Never mind a full-body blush, I'm burning up in hellfire right now. Eyes glassy, I stammer, "N-no, No. Oh my God. *No.*"

I wrench it from his hands, repeating *no* until one of us stands a chance at believing it. My frantic movements and shaky voice are enough to scare off Half-Pint.

"You're too good at drawing to convince me that's anybody else, baby. Besides, that's a normal—albeit *pretty*—cock you drew there. Definitely not an alien dick." Lucas sits sideways on the couch, running a palm up my bare thigh.

My insides are broiling. This must be how spontaneous combustion happens. Good way to go out, honestly.

His voice cuts through the hazy air. "Hey, please don't feel embarrassed. That's so fucking hot. *Shit*, I'm ready and willing to pay some big money to have that printed for my own bedside table."

"This is the fucking worst." I will myself not to cry over this, shoving the tablet under a throw pillow and looking anywhere but at him. "I can't believe you saw that."

"If you'd been standing at my door with that picture in your hands on the first night, I wouldn't have slept on the couch like a gentleman, that's for damn sure."

My fingers squeeze the bridge of my nose so hard it's a wonder it doesn't break. "God, can we just move on and pretend this didn't happen? *Please?*"

Cupping my chin, he pulls until my eyes meet his. "Okay, I'll drop it. But seriously, you're wildly talented. Thank you for the glimpse into that beautiful, bizarre penis-filled head of yours."

Chapter Fifteen

Lucas

December 25

S hortly after breakfast, Eira and I take turns using the landline for our obligatory Christmas Day calls to our parents. Plunking down on the bed with an exhale, I run a hand through my hair while waiting to be added to the family conference call.

"Merry Christmas!" Mom shouts into the phone with an ear-piercing shriek.

"Merry Christmas, everybody," I respond, settling on top of my bed and leaning back against the pillows. Admittedly, I'm not thinking about my family right now. I'm thinking about Eira's nails dug into the wood headboard while she rode my face after our talk in the shower last night. The way we rang in the start of Christmas curled around each other, damp from the shower, with my cock deep inside her warmth.

"We miss you here," Mom yells, never understanding that the speakerphone can pick up her voice at a normal volume.

"Miss you guys," Holly cheerfully sings into the phone. "Maybe next year we can all celebrate together."

"Oh, Holls. That would make me so happy." Mom's hands clap together, so jarring that I reflexively yank the phone away from my ear. *Christ. Is this woman sitting on top of the phone?*

My mom and sisters start yapping about family drama passed on from Mom's call with our grandparents earlier this morning. And I pick at my thumbnail, unsure of what contribution I'm bringing to this conversation, exactly. I'm here because it's easier to tough this out than it is to deal with the wrath if I avoid them altogether. But, *fuck*, I'm itching for it to end so I can get back downstairs to Eira.

"How's the ranch, Lukey?" my older sister, Natalie, asks over the wild shouting of her kids in the background.

"It's exhausting. I don't know." My ears perk at a loud crash, followed by Eira lovingly scolding her demon cat. With a small smile, I shake my head. "Lots of shit to get done, honestly. I should go."

"Lucas, you're not working on Christmas, are you?" Mom's clearly taken aback.

"No, I just want to get back to my *quiet* Christmas." As if on cue, my one-year-old niece starts wailing.

"I hate knowing you're alone," my mom says at the same time Natalie calls me Scrooge.

My other sister, Ivy, cackles, and suddenly all three of my siblings are ganging up on me like we're kids again. I love them, but nobody has ever been jealous of me when they find out I'm the only boy in this situation. Two older sisters, one younger. I got shit from all sides growing up.

It's getting so out-of-hand, I'm considering hanging up when my dad chimes in—it's insane he's even bothering to be in the same room, instead of watching television in the basement—to tell them all to shut the fuck up. And a hush falls over everything.

"Seriously, Lucas." Mom's tone turns threatening. "Next year, I'm not leaving you a choice. You can't keep doing Christmas all by yourself."

Meanwhile, I have a beautiful woman wearing nothing but one of my T-shirts in my living room. If they knew, everyone would leave me the hell alone today. But they'd be down my throat tomorrow, and I can't handle that.

"Anyway, I'm gonna go." I hover the phone an inch from my face, waiting for the inevitable protesting from my mother, and silence from my sisters. At least they're relatively honest about their desire for me to leave them to their gossip. "Love you all. Bye."

I hang up before Mom has the chance to argue, then practically fucking skip downstairs to fully embrace Eira's perfect, no-pants holiday.

✳ ✳ ✳ ✳ ✳

Hours pass where neither one of us moves from the couch except for necessary bathroom and refreshment breaks. Mostly we talk about everything and nothing, and sometimes we simply exist in the same space without words. We fill our stomachs with cookies and squares and bars. Both of us are in my shirts, though the one she's wearing looks like a short dress.

When the sunset starts to weigh on the day, I push aside thoughts of Eira leaving in the morning—refusing to let that ruin our perfect evening. We're illuminated by a small lamp next to the couch, and the twinkle of lights winding delicately through tree branches. They shimmer and change colours with a slow pulse, speckling her body in reds and greens.

"Oh, gosh." Eira holds a flattened palm over her mouth, frantically trying to finish the bite of pastry in her mouth. "I almost forgot I have a present for you."

Side-eyeing her with a healthy mix of curiosity and worry, I say, "A present? Anything you could've bought for me at the grocery store is something I don't need, I can assure you."

"Way to ruin the surprise. I thought you'd appreciate the novelty reindeer poop chocolates," she shouts as she bounds up the stairs.

I toss a couple logs in the fire while she's gone, shutting the cast iron door with a grating squeal that, unsurprisingly, makes Half-Pint hiss in my general direction. I hiss back at her, sticking my tongue out for extra emphasis.

"Did I just interrupt something?" Eira laughs from the doorway.

I hook a thumb toward the spawn of Satan curled up on a couch pillow Eira insisted I could afford to give up. "She started it."

"Close your eyes." Leaning against the door frame, she pops a hip with her hands tucked behind her back. Somehow even prettier than ever before with messy hair, no makeup, and my oversized Coors Banquet T-shirt.

"Yes, ma'am." I do as I'm told.

From so close to me I can smell the lingering aroma of her body wash, she says, "Okay, open."

And there I am. In the barn a couple days ago, shoeing an old bay mare—a retired barrel horse who loves working with little girls, in particular, because they constantly play with her mane.

I know it's me and that Eira drew it, but it looks like it belongs on the wall of a massive art gallery.

"Eira, holy shit. I-I... I don't even know what to... *Wow*."

"I think it might be my favourite piece I've ever done." She smiles down at it, pride radiating from her like sunlight.

"You should keep it then. Something for you to remember this week by."

"No way. I made it specifically for you." She delicately places it on my lap, both of us appreciating the fine details, right down to the hoof trimmings littering the cement floor and the sweat beading along my hairline. "Besides, I have...others."

"This is by far the best gift ever, so thank you." I reach out for her hand, wedging it in my calloused grip.

She smiles, slipping between my knees. "You've gotten a lot of shitty gifts then."

"Fuck any other gift. This is all I want." I dance my fingers up her arm, gliding them to caress her face. "You're all I want."

With candy cane coffee kisses, Eira presses my body against the back of the couch so she can straddle me, plucking the art from my grasp and setting it safely aside.

"I'm all you want?" Her forehead meets mine, dark-brown locks of hair curtaining our faces.

"The best Christmas gift, hands down. The drawing is a very close second."

A slow inhalation to enjoy her scent, a slow exhalation so I can do it all over again.

"I'm going to tell my family to pack it in, because nobody gives as good of gifts as Eira Davies."

"You should probably unwrap your other present before you decide how good of a gift giver I am."

"Reindeer poop chocolates?" A forceful huff of laughter blows from my nose.

"No, but I'm regretting not buying them. Honestly, they looked delicious."

Rocking her hips against my thighs, Eira grabs the hem of her shirt and shimmies it up a few inches.

A shiny red bow sits atop her thin, cotton panties. I toy with it between my fingers, kissing her, swallowing the small whimpers rolling off her tongue.

"You're definitely my favourite gift. *Fuck, baby*. I can't wait to unwrap this."

"It's yours whenever you want it."

This time tomorrow, she'll forever be the one that got away. Knowing my fate before it happens kills me.

Would she view my pleading for her to stay as romantic or insane?

I tuck her hair behind her ears, moving to cradle her skull so I can lose myself even deeper in her kiss.

"You could stay... until the new year... if you want," I softly mutter between the repeated crush of her lips on mine. Tension ripples through my jaw and neck as I wait for the answer I already know is coming.

"I have to go back to work." The way her voice cracks at the end stills the breath in my lungs. Her warm palm presses to my chest, forehead falling against mine again.

"Yeah, I know," I respond hoarsely.

"Let's talk about this at 11:59, okay?" She grabs the bottom of my shirt and slowly slides it, waiting for me to cooperate by pulling my arms through. Then she bends to kiss her way across my clavicles, hands gripping and teasing the length of my torso, and she whispers into the crook of my neck, "God, you're so fucking gorgeous."

She was right to shut down the conversation. We agreed to enjoy this for as long as it lasts. So I reach under the well-worn cotton shirt and cup her breasts, smoothing my thumbs over peaked nipples. Bracing her body for the quiver as I trail my fingertips along the soft curve of her waist then under the waistband.

"Can I have my present now, baby?"

Breathless, she nods, entire body tightening in anticipation. Her ass lifts up just enough for our frenzied hands to work together to slide my jeans and her panties to the floor.

She's already wet, clit slightly swollen and not finding enough friction from the slow rock of her hips on mine. I can help with that, though. I'd make teasing her to orgasm my full-time job, if I could.

My cock presses painfully inside the restrictive fabric of my boxer briefs, only made worse when she grinds her soaking pussy over the bulge. Within seconds, she's making my dick wet through the fabric, and I'm no more than three more sensual gyrations away from blowing it in my pants.

"Give me a second," I say, easing her from my lap. "Can't have you falling off the couch again."

The plaid blanket she cloaked herself in to draw the other night's still hanging off the back of the armchair, and I neatly lay it out in front of the Christmas tree. A gentle tap of my hand has her crawling across the floor with the sleek grace of a prowling predator, coming to sit in the centre of the blanket.

Lit with a kaleidoscope of reds and greens from the twinkling lights, Eira's beauty continues to amaze me. She leans back on her elbows, getting comfortable, and her hair falls messily to one side then the other as she angles her gaze to get a read on me.

"Merry Christmas, baby." I stroke the delicate skin of her inner thighs.

"Merry Chris—*oh my God.*" A moan interrupts her mid-sentence when I lean in to feast on her sugar-sweet pussy. Turns out, not wearing pants and doing nothing but eating is *exactly* how I want to spend every holiday from here on out.

Spine lifting from the blanket, she frantically knots a hand in my short hair, demanding I continue. Quick circles, languid licks, even the occasional nibble. I take the time to thoroughly enjoy my gift, bringing her to the brink of orgasm then letting her go. Over and over, until even a miniscule breeze sends goosebumps down her arms.

"Oh, fuck." She writhes under my touch. "*Yes.* Don't stop. I'm so close." Some variation of swearing and saying my name and insisting I keep going continues until her skin's humming, pussy clenching hard around the gentle thrust of my fingers.

"Remember what I asked for this year? Let it go, baby."

Burying my fingers in her tight cunt, I moan against her clit, doing whatever I can to avoid the embarrassment of coming before either of us have even touched it. That's the kind of shit that makes women feel powerful and proud the first time, but I'm sure the more it happens, the less impressive it gets.

Eira's squeezing my knuckles together, taking what belongs to her, while moans carry through the humid room. "Lucas, *please.*"

My forearms hold the thighs threatening to crush my skull at bay, and the girl of my fucking dreams comes all over my face. Waves of pleasure racking her body, leaving her trembling and encouraging my addiction.

Nobody will ever measure up to this woman for me. I'd hock a loogie in the face of a supermodel for the chance to kiss Eira. I'd give up my entire life for the feel of her pussy. I'd do anything—*any fucking thing*—she asked for the chance to have her in my arms every day.

Maybe that's insane. My family would say I'm being irrational and impulsive and obsessive and... *I don't care.*

Eira fists my hair, pulling me to her for a slow kiss, and she moans when our lips meet; she's enjoying the taste of herself on my tongue as much as I am. Her heels press to my ass, spurring me on.

"That illustration you made..." My nose traces her jaw from the tip of her perfect, rounded chin to the shell of her ear. "The one of us—"

"I thought we weren't talking about it anymore." She angles her neck so I can kiss her pulse point; her racing heartbeat feeding my ravenous desire.

"Hear me out," I whisper against her skin, feeling her hum of disagreement travel the length of her throat. "You lying naked in front of the tree looks even better in real life than it does on paper. There's tinsel on the tree... And I want nothing more than to make your Christmas fantasies come true."

Chapter Sixteen

Eira

The warmth of his breath on the small patch of skin behind my ear makes my heart stutter.

"Come on, baby. Let me give you this."

Shutting my eyes, an answer tumbles out—unconvincing as it may be. "Okay."

I've always been a maladaptive daydreamer, getting so lost in the images my mind conjures I briefly lose sense of reality. To process and move on, I bring my wild imaginings to life through whichever medium best suits. I need the moment when I step back from my art and think *yes, that's exactly what I had pictured it would look like*. Then I'm free to carry on and find a new daydream.

Lucas hands me my iPad, grinning ear to ear as I unlock it. He pulls up the image, glancing over just in time to catch the rosey flush blossom out from my chest.

His eyes study the screen in careful detail, and he holds a smile behind his closed fist. "Fuck, I almost forgot how hot this is."

"Lucas, we don't have to do this if it's too much."

"*Too much?*" He laughs, setting the tablet down and standing to carefully unwind two long strands from the tree. "Baby, there's nothing you could ask me to do that would be too much."

The silver garland sparkles and shines, reflecting the steadily changing coloured light bulbs on nearly every tree branch. He wraps the tinsel around his neck like a scarf as he kneels between my open legs. The crackle of the wood fire has me startling, my nerve endings already on high alert, pulse racing at the thought of what we're about to do.

"You tell me to lick your pussy," he leans in and swipes his tongue up my slit, ending with a small flourish on my clit that sends a vibration through my entire body, "and I'll eat you all fucking night."

He sits back up, cool air blowing across my damp skin at the loss of him.

"You tell me to kiss you?" His lips, still wet with my arousal, softly press to mine. Hovering just above my mouth, he continues to speak. "Baby, I'll kiss you every day for the rest of my goddamn life."

The promise of every day sounds so good, my lips prickle and purse, earning me another honeyed kiss just before he sits back.

"My girl wants to be bound in tinsel?" He smirks, taking hold of my hands. "Fucking hell, I'm going to earn a damn Scouts badge for my knot-tying abilities. I've never done this before... just so you know."

"Neither have I. But... I-I've wanted to."

"If you trust me enough to do this, I promise to take care of you, Eira. I know I got a little"—he scrubs a hand over his jaw, wincing at the memory—"rough before. That won't happen again."

"I trust you." *I really do.*

"If you change your mind, just say tinsel or something. Okay? Something weird and not what you'd normally say while you're coming."

"I'm feeling pretty festive. I *might* start screaming out holiday jargon when I come. You don't know." I swallow hard with the first slip of scratchy plastic garland across my thigh, encircling my shaky muscle.

"You won't," he rasps. "You won't say anything but my name."

Nervous energy buzzes through me, and his focus zeroes in on the delicate twisting, knotting, and looping of tinsel—probably harder to make knots with than rope. The feathered ends tickle my bare skin in a way that elevates every graze of his fingertips. In a matter of seconds, he pulls my wrist tight against my thigh, and I involuntarily suck a sharp inhale through my teeth.

"Too tight?" He stops moving, eyes leaving the knotted garland for the first time since he started this process.

"Um... no." I wave my hand to show there's no pinching where it's held tight just above my knee. I don't have much wiggle room, but knowing I'm unable to pull free has my chest heaving. The tendons in my groin pull taut, creating extra heat and a stretching sensation that hurts so good. "I'm good. *So good.*"

"I already know this is going to be the best fucking thing I've ever done." He plucks the second strand from his neck and begins the same process on my left side.

When he sits back to admire his work—take in the way I'm spread before him like a fucking Christmas dinner—his Adam's apple bobs heavily in his throat, and he lets out a drawn-out exhale.

"Holy shit, Eira. Holy fucking shit." His touch grazes my inner thigh, and I jostle in place at the already heightened sensation. Lucas tucks his thumbs into the waist of his boxer briefs, sliding them down without taking his eyes off me. "You feel good about this still? Tinsel, remember?"

"Yeah, I remember." I lick my lips. Never mind my own pleasure, there's something about the carnal look in his eye and the twitching of his fully erect cock. I'm having this effect on him. This insanely gorgeous, funny, god of a man is close to becoming feral, unravelling entirely, at the mere sight of my naked body.

That feels fucking good.

A moan barrels from my chest when his tongue makes direct contact with my clit. My back arches, thighs immediately moving to grip his skull.

His massive palms spread my legs wide once again. "Be a good girl and keep these open so I can eat."

Whether it's my hands or my thighs that seem to move by their own free will, it's hard to say, but as soon as he has me cresting that peak again, my thighs squeeze together in a last-ditch effort for friction. He swats at my skin, the rap of his knuckles stinging my inner thigh.

"As badly as I want to die between your legs—that can't happen tonight. I'm gonna have to do something about this." He bites my fleshy thigh. "Maybe I should tie them up some more?"

His eyes wander the room, falling on his discarded pants, and in a flash he's ripping the belt away. It snaps in his hands, and he waits for my nod of approval before gliding the smooth leather around my ankle. In a sharp jolt, my leg careens toward the Christmas tree.

"Are you tying me to the tree?"

"Better stay still, baby, or this whole thing is toppling down on us." He smirks, fastening the belt buckle around the tree's base. "Can you keep this leg under control, or am I going to have to start moving furniture around to find an anchor for it?"

"I got it." *I think.*

Not trusting me, the weight of his forearm falls to my thigh, pressing the tinsel into my skin—forcing me to do nothing but sit back and accept pleasure.

Pleasure it certainly is. His tongue starts slow, building in both tempo and pressure, until my breathing happens in short bursts and my back curves against the blanket. Like sinking into a hot bath after a long day, I melt into the orgasm. The binding hugs my flesh, providing just enough support to allow my muscles to relax deeper into the forced stretch.

His tongue continues circling my clit like he's signing his name over and over. Honestly, he may as well be. He already owns me.

"You're doing so well, pretty girl." His lips press to the quaking muscle in my thigh then the sharp points of teeth drag over it, and he laughs under his breath at my gasp. "I love finding new trigger points for you."

"What?" I whimper.

"The different things I can do to get a reaction. Like for instance, you moan when I do this." Two fingers disappear deep inside my vagina and, what do you know, a moan claws its way up my throat.

He pulls back out as quickly as he filled me, and sucks my wetness from his middle finger.

"And I fucking love the noise you make when I do this," he says before leaning in to give my clit a barely there flick with his tongue. Whatever noise comes out of me cannot be described.

And yet again, there's a new whimpering sound when he presses something to my asshole, teasing the opening gently, with a grin sweeping his face. "That's a really fun one. If we had more time, I'd love to see what you'd do with my cock filling this tight hole."

He presses the head against it, letting the slight twitch of his erection rub against my puckered skin until I'm squirming. Not that I've ever trusted a man enough to tie me up before, but if I had, I'm not sure I'd trust anyone else to toe the line of rubbing his cock over my asshole without trying to slide it in when I'm compromised.

Instead he shifts gears, rocking his hips to glide his shaft between my pussy lips, coating himself in my cum. He groans at the sensation, grabbing hold of my hand as he does it again.

"I like hearing your reactions, too." I squeeze his fingers. "Like the noise you made when I sucked your cock into my mouth."

I might've said too much.

"You liked that?" He moves to straddle my chest, hard cock bobbing in front of my lips, which I suddenly realize are sore and swollen from rubbing against my teeth the entire time he devoured me.

"Open up, baby." The smooth, ruddy head parts my lips, and he feeds me inch after inch, until I'm practically choking on him. Part of me considers tapping out as drool seeps from the corners of my mouth. Until he thrusts forward with that fucking sob I love, and I want to make this so good for him.

With slow, deep rolls of his hips, he fucks my mouth, holding one hand in my hair to keep me still. Unable to do anything about the desperate need for friction between my legs, I groan with frustration, shifting my hips and hoping for *anything* to make contact with my clit.

Clearly sensing my need, his free hand reaches behind him to resolve the twinge between my legs. Only he doesn't. He slips around my damp skin, touching everything except where I need.

"You're loving letting me have my way with you, aren't you?"

I mumble the best *uh-huh* I can muster with his large shaft taking up every inch of available real estate in my mouth and throat.

"And you want to come again, don't you?"

The pleading look in my eyes must not be pathetic enough, because Lucas withdraws all but the tip before gliding back in with a grunt.

My irritated exhales around his cock become frantic whimpers when he finally—*fucking finally*—works his fingertips over me.

He stutters a breath, increasing the pressure of his touch. A tingle starts up my thighs. I'm going to come again. Soon.

While my first bound orgasm was relaxing and slow, this one's animalistic. I'm sucking and gulping around him, fighting like hell to break free of the knots dug into my skin. All I want is to throw him off me, climb on top, and ride him until he feels a tiny fraction of the desperation crawling under my skin.

"*That* is my favourite sound—you coming with my cock stuffed in your mouth." In a slow drag, he pulls out of my mouth and shifts off my chest, leaning in to kiss me deeply. My cheeks are sore, lips feel bruised, and I bat my eyelashes at him.

"Are you going to fuck me now?"

"Oh, honey. You said we can't talk about anything important until 11:59. So I'm going to tease you for the next...forty-eight minutes, give or take a couple minutes, and *then* I'll fuck you." He hooks a finger under the tinsel garland, tugging it teasingly. "That should give us just enough time to cut these off, soak your sore body in the bath, and carry you to bed for our chat."

I let out a long sigh. He really is perfect, and I don't think he realizes it. "That sounds like a dream."

"I'm going to take such good care of you tonight. Merry Christmas, baby."

Chapter Seventeen

Lucas

H olding a hand between her skin and the scissors so I don't risk nicking her, I cut the tinsel strings binding her wrists to her thighs. Not that I've been with any women recently, so I don't know if this is the kind of thing they're all into these days, but I'd never thought about tying a woman up for sex.

But seeing her spread wide and completely at my mercy—with fire in her eyes and want painted into every stroke of her tongue over her bottom lip—has my mind reeling with ideas. Not that I know when, or even if, I'll get to do this with her again. But maybe a list of sexy plans will entice her to let me visit occasionally.

"Come on, baby." I help her stand, looping an arm around her waist.

She shakes out the stiffness, giving me a sated look before slowly taking a step forward.

"Thank you for trying that with me," she says as we ascend the stairs. I'm close behind her, keeping a flat hand across her ass, just in case she loses balance in her orgasm-weary state. "That was even better than I thought it would be, honestly. I-I've never... I didn't even know I could come that many times."

I turn the faucet, watching her sink into the tub before there's even an inch of warm water in the bottom. And, as promised, I get right to work rubbing body wash over every exposed inch of skin. Lathering up her arms, shoulders, breasts, stomach. I revel in the small sighs slipping from her lips. She's stunning. Everything from the rich browns of her hair to the permanent creases on her nose from scrunching it as she talks, to the deep cupid's bow that immediately draws your eyes to her plump lips.

"The aftercare definitely solidifies that this place is getting a five star from me," Eira says.

"This review is going to set a lot of expectations that I can't live up to for any future guests."

She narrows her eyebrows at me. "Aftercare is always important, Lucas."

"It's not the aftercare that's the issue. I have a straight up kink for taking care of you, Eira." I shake my head slightly, biting my cheek as I stare down this incredibly frustrating woman. "The problem lies in you making future guests think I'll be fucking them."

"You'd stand to make a lot of money." She shrugs.

I chuckle. "By turning this into a brothel? I bet I would. But I wasn't interested in any women before you, and I damn sure won't want any after."

With a sweep of her hand, she splashes a mixture of water and bubbles up over her chest. "I get that."

The calming lavender aroma mixed with the steady stream of water filling the large tub makes my eyelids heavy. Each blink longer than the last. *I can't be tired*, I think to myself. *We have too many important things to discuss.*

Eira shuts her eyes, sliding deeper into the tub. The tips of her bobbed hair skim the surface of the water when I shut off the faucet, and that's when I realize she's snoring. Lightly. Cutely.

"Baby, hey." I jostle her arm, reaching into the hot bath to pull the plug. "Let's get you to bed, Doodlebug."

Her eyelids flutter to help her adjust to the light, and her yawn reminds me of Half-Pint's annoyed reaction when I checked on her in her box next to the wood stove before we came upstairs.

"I don't wanna go to bed," Eira murmurs like a petulant child, pulling herself out of the tub and letting me wrap a towel around her. "When I wake up in the morning, I have to leave. And I don't want that."

Hearing her admit it guts me. We've skirted around the topic plenty over the course of the day, citing our agreement to wait until the last minute.

It's not quite 11:59 yet, but watching her brush her teeth with hooded eyes, I realize we won't make it to midnight.

Plunking my toothbrush into its holder, I smile at her in the mirror. "I'll come visit you in the city as often as I can."

Her bare feet slap against the tile as she follows me out of the bathroom. "Lucas... I know you can't afford to skip work for me. I don't want you to lose what you've worked so hard for."

"That's not your worry to have. Trust me when I say that a trip to see you, even if it's just for a single evening, is going to be so much better for me than anything here." I tuck her into the covers, sliding in afterward and wrapping my arm around her small body. "Being with you eases all that weight on my shoulders. I'm going to need that from time to time."

"Okay. You can come visit," she says through a yawn. "Just don't go snooping for the other drawings I have of you."

"I definitely won't look in your bedside table drawer the second you turn your back."

Twisting her head to look over her shoulder, she kisses me slowly.

Falling asleep with her secure in my arms, I whisper, "Merry Christmas, beautiful."

＊＊＊＊＊

Morning comes too soon, shattering the illusion that some type of Christmas magic would lead to a snowstorm, highway closure, or sudden layoffs at her job. I tossed and turned through the night, hopeful the clocks might stop. But when the sun reared its ugly head from between the gaping blinds on my window, I knew it was all for nothing.

I stroke her jawline with the back of my fingers, staring at the fanning of dark eyelashes over her cheeks. Even deep in slumber, there's an uptick to the corners of her mouth, like she's fighting to hold back a secret.

For a minute, I consider heading downstairs to cook breakfast again, then decide I'd much rather stay with her for every second we have, even if it means eating cereal.

She stirs, cuddling into me with an adorable grumble as she tucks her hand up next to her cheek. I hold her secure to my side, with slow circles of my hand over her back. Eira mumbles something I don't quite catch against my bare chest, and I try to steal a glimpse of her face to determine if she's talking in her sleep.

"Tell me it's Groundhog Day," she repeats louder. "Tell me I woke up and it's Christmas Day again."

Laughing under my breath, I rest my chin on the top of her head and breathe deeply.

"No such luck, Doodlebug. And you slept in—it's nearly ten o'clock."

Her head shoots up, a flash of fire in her eyes. "You let me sleep in?"

"You needed your sleep. Last night was a lot." Wrapping myself around her, I force her down on top of me. Our chests rise and fall in perfect concert, slowing in the peacefulness of being together.

"I can sleep when I'm dead. I wanted to spend the morning together."

"We still have a bit of time." My attempt at reassurance is undeniably half-assed. She needs to be out of here within the next couple hours so she can get home before sunset—regardless of how badly I want to spend every last second together, I can't have her driving in dark and snowy conditions.

"Yeah…" She smiles up at me. "We have a little bit of time."

Chapter Eighteen

Eira

December 26

I will not cry. I will not cry. I will not cry.

I throw my arms around his neck, kissing him until I lose myself. My fingers raking up the back of his skull, the pull of his hands finding their home on my hips.

Half-Pint circles my ankles, and I bend down to gingerly scoop her up. There's one final nail drag over my knuckles—a gift to remember her by. Risking another injury, I give her a quick peck on the head, weaving out of the way as she turns to bite me.

"Bye, baby. I hope you find a family who loves you as much as I do." Saliva binds up in my throat, aching and burning on the way down with a series of hard swallows. I crinkle my nose, staring down her tiny face, reminding myself of her copper eyes and the few random white whiskers like tiger stripes on her inky face.

Turning to look at Lucas, I ask, "You'll take her to the rescue when they open after the holidays, right?"

My eyebrows narrow as I wait for his answer. I'm half expecting him to bring her right back to the stables we found her at the moment I pull out of the driveway.

"Promised I would, didn't I?" He moves like he's going to pet her, but thinks better of it when she flashes a look in his direction.

With a loud exhale, I set Half-Pint at my feet. "I guess I should go."

Thinking about waking up alone tomorrow, slipping into my uncomfortable office attire and riding the train to a high-rise building so I can sit at a desk all day makes my stomach twist.

"Long drive ahead of you," he says with a nod. "You'll call me when you get there?"

"Promised I would, didn't I?" My chin trembles.

For another few seconds, we both stand in silence, rolling our lips and gnawing on our cheeks. Emotion clings to every gently falling snowflake in the air, and neither of us wants to be the one to pull the trigger—say the official goodbye.

"So... um..." I try to clear the words lodged in my throat with a small cough into my sleeve.

"Should we just go put your stuff back upstairs?" Lucas tilts his head toward the staircase.

God, he's only making it harder to refrain from calling my boss and lying about a dead grandma, or car accident, or illness that'll keep me from work for another week.

Shaking my head with tears brimming my eyes, I say, "I'll call you when I get home."

"And I'll figure something out to come visit you soon."

I don't know that he will. Of course, I'd love it if there was a logical way we could make things work between us, but that four-hour drive may as well be forty. I've pieced together enough between our conversations, Holly's comments about his stress-level, and the fact he's renting out a cabin seemingly against his will—he's probably one missed pay cheque away from losing the things that mean everything to him. I can't, in good conscience, ask him to spend time and money he doesn't have.

But I also can't bring myself to tell him that his words are bullshit.

"I'd love that." I press up onto tiptoes, holding his scruffy face in my hands and kissing him. "Bye, Lucas."

One long, deep, peppermint toothpaste-flavoured kiss later, he murmurs against my lips, "See you later, Doodlebug."

Chapter Nineteen

Eira

January 3

> I just saw a man with a very flat-looking ass getting off the train. Was it you?!

Lucas

If you keep telling me you're checking out other guys, I'll have no choice but to come there

> Almost like that's my plan or something ;)

> It's been a long week being back in the city. So many asses. None of them yours.

Lucas

Better not be adding any of those guys to your drawing spank bank

> Nothing but your not-flat butt and pretty dick, don't worry

> Did you drop off Half-Pint yet?

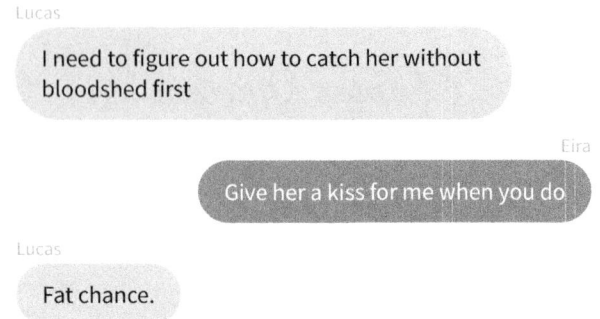

Lucas

I need to figure out how to catch her without bloodshed first

Eira

Give her a kiss for me when you do

Lucas

Fat chance.

The door chimes, and I enter the warm café with an exaggerated shiver. Coffee aroma swirls through the air, and the milk steamer's hiss is louder than the hum of voices in the busy room. I slip between patrons, beelining for our corner table where Holly's already sitting criss-cross in her armchair, resting a steaming mug on her knee.

"Hey, happy belated Christmas," I say, folding my jacket over the back of an empty chair before sinking into it with a sigh.

"You weren't murdered," Holly states the obvious.

"And you sound less than thrilled about it...which I don't love." I pick up the flat white she ordered ahead of time for me, stirring the candy cane around while eyeballing my best friend. "Arsenic or cyanide?"

"Thallium, obviously."

I shoot a finger gun at her with a wink. "The poisoner's poison. Good choice. How was your Christmas? Did you poison your in-laws, too?"

She blows on her hot drink before taking a careful sip. "It was good, Daniel's brother was there with his family. We ran this ridiculous Santa 5K on Boxing Day where a ton of people dressed as Santa."

I smile to myself, immediately starting a mental countdown timer until I can text Lucas about the running-family's Christmas activity. We text as often as we can during work hours, and he calls me every night. Generally, there's a light-hearted, teenagers-in-love style argument about who's hanging up first when it's time for bed.

"How about you? You look completely refreshed—or like you had Botox. Everything seems...*lifted* or something." Holly's fingers circle wildly around her face, pointing to nothing and everything all at once. "Take it your time away was good? Tell me all your thoughts on the cabin."

I choke on air, frantically clutching my coffee and easing into a small sip. All at once, the room is unbearably hot and my clothes are too tight. Holly's engagement ring taps against the side of her mug as she eagerly awaits my answer.

I knew this question would come. I just can't bring myself to tell the elaborate lie I made up on my drive back from Fox Ridge.

"Well, the uh...wood stove was an issue. Consider yourself lucky I didn't have cell reception, because there's no way we'd still be friends after the choice words I had for you."

"*Shit.*" Her entire face scrunches. "Should've known that would be a problem. Lucas and I argued before about getting an electric baseboard heater or something as backup, but I'll try harder to convince him we need it. *Fuck.*"

The thought of him spending more money on the cabin because of me nearly makes me ill.

"I would hold off. It was definitely just me being an idiot. Maybe print out some *super* simple instructions, in case somebody else is as bad at survival skills as I am. Plus, once it's lit, it's easy to keep going."

"Okay, yeah... yeah, it'll be spring before we know it, anyway. Maybe before next winter we'll invest in something else. Any other critiques?"

The lukewarm coffee scalds its way to my stomach. Or maybe it's the lie slowly poisoning me.

"Nope. The cabin's beautiful." *Not a lie.* "And you'll be shocked to know I didn't fully detest the snow." *Also not a lie.*

"Did you see my brother at all?"

In an effort to prevent my eyes from becoming the size of Half-Pint's food bowl, I act like there's an eyelash in one, blinking rapidly and shooting my gaze down toward the floor. I'm sure I look crazy, but I wasn't expecting to get *grilled* like this.

"Well, yeah, actually." I think I might be having a heart attack—this chest pain and breathlessness doesn't seem right. Would be a convenient way out of the conversation, though.

And Holly doesn't seem the least bit phased by my caginess. "Did he seem okay? Mom's been worried about him since we had our family conference call on Christmas. He acted extra eager to hang up, and then I guess when she called him on Boxing Day, he didn't answer at all."

Goddamnit, Lucas. I hope we suddenly developed telepathy, and he hears the mental cussing out I'm doing. Because he couldn't just have a nice, healthy conversation with his mom, I'm now forced to choose between letting his family continue to worry, or admitting to my best friend that the reason her brother was eager to hang up the phone was so he could bind my limbs with tinsel.

"Holls..." I chew incessantly on my thumbnail. "He, um... He seemed fine."

Can't wait to see how hot the flames are in hell.

"I told Mom he was probably just exhausted and stressed from working so much lately." She shrugs casually then dives into a long rant about a conversation she recently had with her wedding photographer.

And I feel like a shitty friend when my focus wanders almost immediately. I can't help that there's a couple cozied up in the coffee line and it makes my mind drift to Lucas again.

"You hang up," I whispered sleepily, eyes already shut and growing harder to open with each passing second.

"No, you," he said through a yawn.

I laughed. "We're like a couple of teenagers."

"And our parents grounded us for fucking under the Christmas tree, so now we can't see each other for a while."

"Exactly." I tucked the comforter tighter around my chin. *"I love our discreet prison calls."*

Except that it was starting to feel like a life sentence.

"Me too, Doodlebug. I'll come see you soon."

Mere days since I'd left the ranch, and he'd mentioned visiting me no less than twenty times. I knew his intentions were genuine, but the more I heard it, the less I believed it would ever happen.

The slam of the café's glass door snaps my attention back to the present. Back to where Holly's still rambling about a "first look" for their wedding.

Somehow the fact that Lucas and I will be in the wedding party together in five short months skipped our minds. Granted, it's so far away, I suppose having a conversation about how we'll approach that situation would be a bit premature. Who's to say what things between us will look like by the time the wedding rolls around. I did the college spring break bullshit when I was younger—I've spent more than five days shacked up in a hotel room with a guy before, and it never led to anything. Maybe this won't be any different.

Except Lucas is different. *Better.*

With him, I'm home.

"I guess my point is... *elope.* This experience so far is about a seven out of ten on the stress scale." Holly cradles her mug in front of taupe painted lips, stopping just shy of taking a sip. "Tell me something good. Any wacky dick pics? Maybe a penis inside a sub sandwich?"

I snort. "No, thankfully. Love that size of dick in my monster smut, but I'd run for the hills in real life."

"Yeah, nobody wants to have a man literally rearrange their organs." She cringes. "You always have freaky dating stories, so give me *something*."

"I always have stories because you're usually picking the guys for me," I point out. "And I haven't seen you in a couple weeks."

"Did you open the app in Fox Ridge?"

I didn't. "Yeah... nothing but men holding up fish that were varying degrees of impressive."

"*Fish?*"

I nod emphatically, raising a closed fist as if I'm dangling a giant trout next to my face. "Fish."

I don't actually know if that's true for Fox Ridge, though I'm pretty confident in my conviction. I've seen enough women lamenting online about their dating prospects in small towns like that.

"Weird." She holds a hand out, fingers clapping against her palm. "Let's see what new guys we can find in the city."

Like I was just body slammed by the huge finance bro waiting in line for his triple espresso a few feet away, all the wind is knocked from my chest.

"Oh, well..." I gulp. "I deleted the app."

"The fish men turned you off *that* badly?"

"No," I say through an awkward laugh. "Holls, I actually met somebody really great, and I don't know if it will ever—*could ever*—be something real. But..."

I want to try.

Holly's face lights up. "We've been here for twenty-five minutes and this is the first you're telling me about this? Who is he? How did you meet? Please don't tell me it's the hot dog guy. Like... I'm not *opposed* to a hot dog bar at your future wedding, but just know I'll never be able to look at your husband and keep a straight face."

"First of all, it's *not* our Oscar Meyer buddy. Secondly, cool your jets because I literally just told you it's nothing serious, and you're already talking catering."

She wags a finger at me. "To be fair, I might be onto something with the hot dogs. That sounds a lot more affordable than what our caterer is charging."

The teensiest part of my brain wishes I could just tell her I'm dating the hot firefighter who sent me the questionable dick pic before Christmas. We'd have a laugh—*at my expense*—and move on like normal. At least there would be no risk to our friendship.

"So, tell me about this guy."

"We met a while back actually, but just, um, had the chance to reconnect. He's nice... funny." I'm stalling, and she knows it. She takes a bite of muffin, rolling her free hand to encourage my bean-spilling as she chews.

"Holls... it's Lucas."

And that's the moment I kill my best friend.

Almost.

She chokes on the banana oat muffin, shrapnel spraying from her mouth in an unavoidable coughing fit. Frantically, she reaches for a drink, and I meet her halfway, handing the cup to her. I watch her chug coffee with tear-filled eyes and lungs that are fighting to function. While my own blueberry scone is sitting safely on the table, I'm still struggling to speak, thanks to the obtrusive uvula blocking my throat.

"*Lucas?*" she croaks, finally able to utter a single word between coughs. "My... brother?"

"I know, I know. I'm the worst friend." I wince, waiting for an indication that she agrees with my statement.

But Holly's staring at me in a sweetly similar way to how she eyes up the Sipsters bakery case.

"I *swear* I didn't go to the ranch with any intentions."

"Yes, you did," she counters. "You said you reconnected. So there was a whole-ass 'connection' before that you failed to mention."

Shit, I did say that, didn't I?

"You saw us talking at the bar during your engagement party. That's the connection."

"Okay, so... shit, *really?* My brother, Lucas? Are you sure?"

"Yes, Lucas," I say with a smile that I can't help anytime I think about him. "Tell your mom I'm really sorry he worried her on Christmas. We were together, and I think he didn't trust me and Half-Pint not to destroy the house. That's why he was so eager to leave."

She blinks rapidly at me. "Half-Pint?"

"The kitten we rescued out at the—"

Pinching the bridge of her nose, she interrupts. "You *share* a cat?"

"We just saved her from freezing to death, but he's taking her to the shelter today. They were closed over the holidays."

"So you're, like, fully together? How is that going to work?"

My anxiety-driven racing pulse and clammy hands turn into melancholia. With an intense quiver in my bottom lip, my voice cracks when I open my mouth.

"I d—I don't know, Holls. He keeps promising he'll come visit, but with the situation at the ranch, it's too much for me to ask *when exactly* he plans to do that."

"Nah, it's not too much to ask."

"He wants to... I know he wants to come see me."

"If he wanted to, he would." She's practically shouting, her hands clapping together to punctuate each word, causing the neighbouring table of twenty-something girls to look our way and give a hurrah in solidarity.

Sometimes I really love women.

"Okay, okay. You're right."

"Always am." She sits back, crossing her arms over her chest and adjusting the sleeves of her wine-coloured sweater. "I'm actually really annoyed with myself for not thinking of this. You two just seemed so unlikely, given your entirely different lifestyles. But clearly finance bros and tech guys in the city aren't doing it for you." After mulling it over for a second, she adds, "You know what? I *am* going to take credit for this, actually, since I convinced you to go to the ranch for Christmas."

Her priorities definitely add up here.

"You're not pissed I didn't tell you sooner?"

"Well, yeah, *duh.* If you'd told me, I could've found a million sneaky excuses to force that reconnection months earlier than I did."

My heartbeat's slowly returning to normal, thanks to the genuine—albeit somewhat conniving—smile on my best friend's face.

"I think things were meant to happen the way they did," I say.

"Let me just say, our rule about you showing me every wild dick picture you receive has officially gone out the window. But, *God*, I love this. I love both of you."

"Like I said... It doesn't seem like the type of thing that will ever work out long term. So don't get your hopes up."

"Blah, blah, blah. Get me a hot dog bar at your wedding as a thank you."

Chapter Twenty

Eira

January 29

Lucas

Saw this and thought of you

I accidentally cackle out loud on the train home from work when the picture comes through: a mug covered in a pattern of cat butts. An old woman narrows her eyes at me, and I continue to snicker quietly into the collar of my wool coat.

It feels like I should be offended by that…

This crosses the line, but not the flat-assed dude pictures you send me all the time?

Speaking of which… You sure this isn't you?

I fire off the picture then slip my phone into my pocket and step through the open train doors at my stop. The evening breeze has a bite to it that makes me pull my coat up over my ears, wishing I'd worn a scarf. Despite the dark sky, there's not a star in sight, and I trudge along the slushy sidewalk.

The snow's melting thanks to Canada's infamous false-spring, where naive souls—such as myself—get our hopes up during a random bout of warm weather in late January. All so the Earth can turn around with a big *fuck you* in the form of a blizzard, like the one I'm willing to bet comes next week.

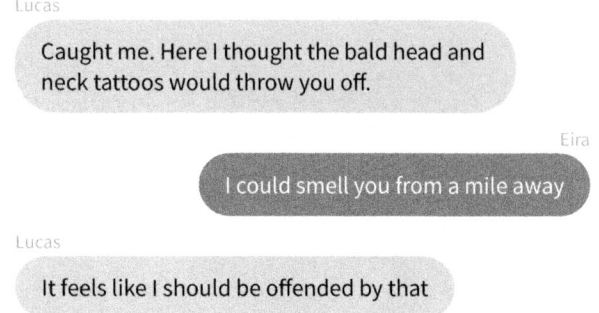

Lucas

Caught me. Here I thought the bald head and neck tattoos would throw you off.

Eira

I could smell you from a mile away

Lucas

It feels like I should be offended by that

I could tell him it's a compliment. That I bought a candle last week simply because the scent when I walked through the store brought me crashing back to his bed, breathing in the smell of his warm skin. That I turn my candle warmer on every night so my room smells like him when I fall asleep.

Or that I went back two days ago and bought ten more of the same candle, just in case they discontinue them.

For the last month we've been talking almost non-stop during waking hours, between text messages all day and phone calls at night. But we flirt, we talk about our day, and we don't talk about anything important. Like what the fuck we're doing here, or why he still hasn't come to visit.

Lucas

I can taste you from almost 500km away, snow angel

Eira

Yeah? What do I taste like?

Lucas

Mine.

Chapter Twenty-One

Lucas

February 19

I switch up the grip on my rasp, spinning it to slide the handle into a loop on the side of my tool belt. I'm not usually an eavesdropper, but my ears perk up hearing the stable manager and lead therapeutic riding instructor chatting at the end of the alley.

"Hey," I call out, dropping the pastern and standing to look toward the two women. "Sorry to startle you. I heard you talking about wanting to make some pamphlets or something for the kids camp."

"Uh..." The stable manager's eyes flit from me, to her trainer, then back. "Yeah, we want some kid-friendly booklets about horse care, riding, that kind of thing."

"My g—I know a *really* talented illustrator."

"You do?" Crystal, the lead trainer, raises an eyebrow.

"I do. She doesn't usually illustrate this type of stuff." Heat rises in my cheeks at the recollection of Eira's drawings. "But she's so talented, I'm sure she could do it. I'll text you her contact info."

"Incredible. Um... thanks, Lucas?"

With a silent nod, I head back to the senior mare waiting for me to finish her back left foot.

> You okay with me passing on your number for some potential illustration work?

Eira

> Did you finally find that rich art gallery owner you mentioned?

Lucas

> Not exactly. The stable wants some kids books made up about basic horse care.

> Less thrilling than drawing me naked, I'm sure. But one commission closer to full-time illustrating.

Eira

> Yes, please. You don't know how badly I needed that kind of good news today

Sending her a lengthy chain of heart emojis, my own falls heavy into my gut. I hate knowing she's having a hard day and, even though we'll talk on the phone tonight, I can't be there to pour her a glass of bourbon and run her a hot bath. I can't be there.

Fuck, I hate that.

※ ※ ※ ※ ※

The house is dark and desolate when I pull my truck into the driveway. A light on in the cabin catches my eye, and I let out an involuntary huff when the car parked outside clearly isn't Eira's. It never is, but I can't help myself from feeling a tiny speck of hope every time. Holly's secured a fair number of bookings, and as annoyed as I am about occasionally having to help with the wood stove or get a car without proper tires unstuck from the end of the driveway, the income's chipping away at the weight on my shoulders. If she's right, it'll be even busier during the spring and summer months, and I won't need to stress about feeding animals next winter regardless of the hay supply.

A small black cat sits in the big living room window, and she stretches her front paws along the windowsill when she sees me coming up the steps. A resounding, "you're late" meow blares through the quiet home before I've even had the chance to take off my shoes. Then suddenly she's purring and circling my feet.

"Oh, bullshit. You're sucking up because I'm late feeding you dinner."

Another meow. Sassier.

It's a challenge to walk to the kitchen without tripping over her, since she insists on weaving between my legs. In a past life, she might've been a herding dog.

"Cool your jets. You and I both know you won't touch the kibble if I don't add that foul wet stuff first. If I fall and break my wrist, you'll be fucked since you lack the ability to use a can opener."

Her meows grow louder with every passing second, and I shoot a glare at her, taking my sweet fucking time dishing up the grub. When the bowl clangs on the floor, the devil cat nearly takes my hand off to get at it. I gave her extra wet food tonight, knowing she's one to hold a grudge about me getting home late.

I grab my phone and lean against the counter. Gnawing my cheek, I stare at my realtor's contact profile, debating throwing all this away to chase after her. Given my tendency to throw caution to the wind and fly by the seat of my pants, I'm probably the only person who would be surprised by me suddenly uprooting my life.

I've never changed my life plans—or made new ones—because of a woman. But I've said before that I'd bet the farm on Eira Davies. And now I'm prepared to make good on that. I just need to figure everything out discreetly before I say a word to her, because making a promise as big as this one will absolutely break her heart if it doesn't work out.

Chapter Twenty-Two

Eira

March 18

B ack in my Laura Ingalls roleplay mindset, I flit through the apartment, ensuring everything is perfect. I squint at the fresh-cut flowers sitting in a vase on my tiny table—adjusting them until they look like something from a magazine—fluff pillows on the couch, and ensure my sexiest drawing is at the top of the pile in my nightstand, all while never leaving the soup unattended for longer than two minutes at a time. None of these things likely matter, considering I don't anticipate leaving the bed for the entire forty-eight hours he's here. Not after waiting so *freaking* long to be with him again.

Two and a half of the slowest-moving months of my entire life.

No amount of text messages, phone calls, or FaceTimes would ever be enough to replace the feeling of Lucas's thick arms around my body when he hauls me into his lap and kisses me like he's starved for the taste of my lips. Which is *exactly* what will be happening in approximately four hours, fifty-six minutes, and thirty seconds... give or take a few minutes.

Determined not to mess up the soup, I take to calling Holly instead of jumping into my latest book cover project. At least she's a human capable of reminding me to check on the boiling pot if I forget.

"Hey, babe," Holly says. "Change your mind about coming to the concert tonight?"

"Nope. Lucas should be here just in time for dinner, and I'm attempting a redo of the soup I failed to make at the ranch." I fill a glass with water and lean against the counter with an exhale. I have no idea how women survived back in the day—taking care of a house and cooking a big meal is *exhausting*.

"Well, hey, if you guys decide to leave your bed for a couple hours, let me know. We have the entire box to ourselves." By the tone of her voice, I can sense the ear-to-ear grin. She's only been looking forward to this Keely James concert for *months*, and I had planned to be there until Lucas told me he could finally come visit.

I laugh nervously under my breath. "It's been so long since he and I saw each other in person. What if it's different now?"

"You never stop talking about him. He never stops talking about you," she says. "That's not going to be an issue."

"Yeah..."

"I'm sensing a but."

"We've barely had the chance to talk for the last couple weeks. Not for lack of trying on my part." I chew the inside of my cheek for a moment. "I know he's really busy, so I'm trying hard not to assume the worst. But just... What if he's trying to push me away?"

"Get out of your own head, Eira. He wouldn't be taking time out of his crazy schedule to visit if he didn't want to be with you."

She's right. Of course she's right. The text messages are more spaced out because we're both so busy with work. The phone calls dwindled to a couple nights per week because we're both exhausted all the time. And the FaceTimes have stopped because there's no time for phone sex when we're lucky to have more than two minutes to chat.

"That's true. I think we just need this weekend to get back on track."

"Long distance is hard," Holly agrees. "But just think, next month we have the wedding shower, which he'll be here for.

Then in May he has to come to the city for both the bachelor party and the wedding. So you'll get plenty of time with my brother."

I open my mouth to say something at the same moment a call from Lucas comes through. "Oh, shit. He's calling me right now. Thanks for talking me down. I expect a million videos from the concert tonight. Make me feel like I was there, all right?"

"You'll be thoroughly spammed, don't you worry," she says just before the dull beep indicates she's hung up.

I melt—all anxiety leaving my body—the instant his deep, gravelly voice hits my ears with a, "hey, baby."

Smiling into the phone and twirling a lock of hair around a fingertip, I feel like a preteen girl talking to her first crush. And I fucking love it.

"Please tell me you're on your way." I grab a tea towel and squeeze it tight in my fingers, waiting with bated breath for his answer. If he says yes, it means he'll be here even earlier than expected.

"Doodlebug, I'm so fucking sorry."

The towel falls to the floor, and I nearly go with it.

"You're...you're not coming, are you?" I fight the urge to cry, emotion clung to every word, saliva pooling in my mouth.

"I wanted to so fucking bad, Eira. Honest."

My lip quivers, and I bite down until the physical pain nearly outweighs the emotional anguish.

"I just can't get away from this place this weekend. I had something come up, and I tried to move it but..." Admittedly, there's a small shred of joy in my soul when his words trail off because his voice is too shaky to finish. I probably shouldn't feel comforted by his pain, but hurting together is better than wondering if I'm alone in my anguish.

"It's okay." *No, it's not.* "I understand." *No, I do not.*

"I'm going to make this up to you, I promise."

I turn off the burner to slow the roll of the boiling broth. Based on the way my stomach's already twisting itself into tight knots, I'm not eating anything tonight anyway. With a focused breath, I shut my eyes and don't bother stopping the tears building in the corners.

"I-I really wanted to see you," I say softly. "I miss you."

"God, I miss you *so* much. It's killing me not to be coming there. I can't stand it."

"Lucas…" My voice breaks for good. I don't even know what I was about to say. What can I even say in this situation? *Give your dreams up for me because I think I'm in love with you?*

"Please don't cry," he pleads. "*Please*. I swear, I'll come visit as soon as I can."

"I know." My face scrunches in agony. "It's okay. I'll go to that country concert with Holly tonight instead. And I'll call you tomorrow like normal, right?"

"*Fuck*. Um… yeah, but can it wait until tomorrow night? I have some important ranch business I need to handle during the day."

Sighing, I nod despite knowing he can't see me. "Sure, tomorrow night. I… uh, guess I better go get ready for the concert."

"Have fun, baby. I miss you so much."

My knees buckle at the precise moment I end the call, and I remain nothing but a lump on the kitchen floor for the next hour. The concert was simply an excuse to hang up before I said something I didn't mean. Or, *worse*, something I *do* mean.

Sobbing into my knees, arms wrapped around myself, I question every interaction we've had lately. Plucking figurative daisy petals in my mind. *Does he love me? Does he love me not?*

And when I've peeled myself from the floor, barely dragging my broken heart down the hall to the bathroom, I strip the cute loungewear from my fully shaved and exfoliated body, and cry my eyes out in the bath.

The water barely covers half of my body, leaving me shivering despite the hot water, and I can't help but think of Lucas's rough hands holding a small, soft washcloth as he sweetly cleaned my skin. I can't reasonably ask him to throw away his entire life, and all the things he's worked so hard for, because I would give anything to see his smile, feel the warmth of his hands on my skin, and taste the sweetness of his lips on a daily basis.

I would give anything...

Fate brought us together twice before, but I can't sit back and naively expect it to realize we're idiots who need repeated meet-cutes to help us stay together. I have to take it into my own hands and find a way to show him how good we are together. Give him reason to believe we can make it.

Chapter Twenty-Three

Lucas

March 25

I toss a hay bale over the paddock fence and yank my phone from my pocket. My sister's obnoxious personalized ringtone has gone off no less than four times in the last half hour.

"Fucking Christ, Holly. This better be an emergency." I wipe a bead of sweat from my eyebrow and start the trek back toward the hay shed. The piece-of-shit skidsteer broke *again*, so I'm hand-bombing hay out to every animal on the property. Flames lick at the muscles in my back with each movement, and my shirt's drenched in sweat despite the cool temperature.

"Oh, it's about to be if I have to drive out there and wring your neck."

I reach for my water bottle sitting on the fence post to pour equal amounts into my mouth and overtop of my head. "What for now?"

"Eira," she spits into the phone.

Her name clobbers my heart with a steel pipe. I already know I'm fucking things up with her—praying it'll be worth it if she sticks this out for a while longer.

"This isn't a good time to get a lecture from you."

"You're going to lose her, Lucas. And I know you don't want to."

She's right on both counts.

Shoving the phone into my T-shirt chest pocket, I heave another bale over my shoulder with a grunt. "You do, do ya?"

"Don't be a dick."

"I'm listing the ranch, all right? Happy now?"

My words are met with rare silence from my younger sister.

"Trust me when I say I wanted nothing more than to see Eira last weekend—and every fucking weekend. But my realtor and lawyer need to go over a bunch of shit with me so we can list it, since the cattle operation is going with it."

I drop the bale to the ground then use the unending silence as an opportunity to shove armfuls of scratchy loose hay into a hay net, kicking the leftovers under the fence rail to my old mare.

"You said you'd never sell it," she eventually says, skepticism layered in her tone. "Are you just listing it to get everyone off your back about it?"

"No. I'm listing it with the intent to sell." I look out at the fog-blanketed mountains, blindly scratching a horse's neck. Sure, I've thought long and hard about this decision for weeks, but it still scares the shit out of me. "It's time for a change of pace."

Chapter Twenty-Four

Eira

March 25

Eira:

> Skipping coffee tomorrow

> Please forgive me

Holly

Bitch, I've got thallium on order for next week already

If everything goes to plan, I won't be there next week either. But I'm not telling her that quite yet.

The Fur-Ever Home Animal Rescue manager, Dolly, slides a mug shaped like a cat across her desk to me. "I'm so glad you could meet me in person. I feel bad you drove all the way here, though."

"It was no problem," I say with a smile. "I was planning to be in the neighbourhood anyway."

I grab the calico tail handle and take a hearty sip while she outlines the project she has in mind. Doing business rebrands, comics, and animal-care graphics aren't my usual project choice, but after creating an illustrated children's book for Fox Ridge Therapeutic Riding a few weeks ago, I've had three animal rescues and a 4-H club reach out.

It's a nice palette cleanser between the alien cocks I've been drawing almost non-stop, thanks to a prolific author going viral with one of my cover designs in January.

I smile up at her as I finish taking notes, underlining the completion date she's requesting. "Thanks so much for asking me to do this. I love cats and helping them in any way I can. But you guys have a special place in my heart... You probably see so many animals, you don't remember them all, but Lucas McKinney brought in a kitten a couple months ago. Any idea how she's doing now?"

Dolly purses her lips in thought. "I don't remember Lucas bringing in any animals recently. He dropped off a dog he found back in the fall, but that's the last I remember."

"Just a small black kitten." I cup my hands together to demonstrate the tininess. "We found her over the holidays, but you were closed, and he said he was going to bring her in afterward."

She shrugs casually. "We haven't had any kittens lately."

Did he bring her back to the barn even though he swore he wouldn't?

Shaking my head to clear it, I smile and reach out for a handshake. "I have to run, or I'll be late meeting my realtor. But thank you again for the opportunity, Dolly. I'm excited to get started on this."

Leaving the shelter, I move like an Olympic champion speed walker down the sidewalk, already late to meet the realtor a few blocks away. The stubby, worn buildings that make up Fox Ridge's singular block of businesses cast a shadow that nips at my skin, and my cold fingertips struggle to type out a coherent text.

Eira

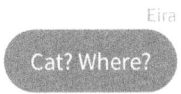

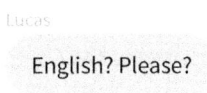

English? Please?

He calls, but I can't answer. Partially because I'm less than a minute away from my destination. Partially because he doesn't know I'm in Fox Ridge, and I'm convinced I'd somehow blow the surprise. As if the second I answer, somebody in the empty street will yell out, *Hey, did you know you're in Fox Ridge?*

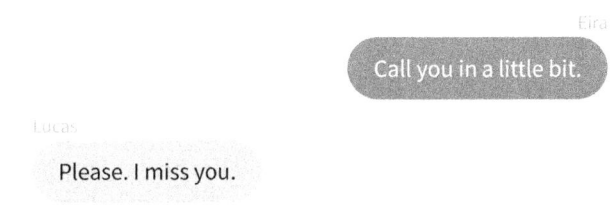

Call you in a little bit.

Please. I miss you.

He is going to shit *when I pull up to the ranch this evening.*

Smiling to myself, I look up at the blue skies and take a deep breath. I'm sure my family and friends will say I'm crazy for uprooting my life on a whim. But after I left Fox Ridge, I nabbed a page out of Lucas's playbook and chose to trust in fate.

And the second I did that, things started falling into place.

He leaned into me outside the bar, filling the already warm summer air with a new, inescapable heat. "I'm so fucking attracted to you in every sense of the word."

"Oh, darn." I licked my lips. "What should we do about that?"

"Tonight? We should go back to my hotel room, and you should let me worship you."

"And after tonight?"

His hand on the small of my back, adding to the mounting ache between my thighs, he ushered me toward the Uber. "We should trust in fate."

"Whatever will be, will be, hey?" I slid into the seat with him hot on my heels. "That sounds like a debonair way of saying you don't plan to call me after tonight."

"Not at all, Doodlebug. I like to think fate gives us the tools—paint, brushes, canvas—and the vision. But it's up to us to create it."

"So, fate is like Bob Ross?" I side-eyed him, warming my palm against his.

He chuckled quietly. "A series of happy little accidents brought us to this moment, didn't they?"

A break in the sidewalk catches the toe of my Chelsea boot, and all reminiscence shatters when I crash to the ground. There's an instant pain in my knee and the heels of my hands, forcing me to sit and collect myself for a moment before I dare stand back up.

"Are you—" Lucas's voice wraps around me. "Eira? What are you doing here?"

"Hey." I smile up at him, blinking back tears. "*Surprise.*"

"Surprise is damn—" He doesn't even let his own sentence leave his lips before they're colliding with mine. In complete contradiction to my racing pulse, his kiss is slow and indulgent. It's welcoming me home, with a languid swipe of his tongue between my parted lips. Pressing on his chest, my hand confirms the rapid thrum of his heart matches my own.

"I... I'm running late," I mumble between kisses.

"For..." *Kiss.* "What?" *Kiss.*

With a hard swallow, I swipe my hand to the back of his neck, revelling in the goosebumps that arise.

"It was supposed to be a surprise...but I quit my job yesterday." I mindlessly straighten the corduroy collar of his denim coat. "And when I was scrolling social media last night, an ad for a real estate agent in Fox Ridge popped up. Thirty minutes of rabbit-holing later, I was booking an apartment showing for today."

Lucas's thumb applies firm pressure to my chin, keeping me locked in place, and his stare is unnerving. "You're moving here."

A statement, not a question.

"Well, I was considering—"

"Let's go see the realtor. Right now. *Come on, baby.*" He excitedly tugs at my arm, stopping immediately when he senses my hesitation. In the heat of the moment, I think he forgot he found me in pain on the ground. He looks down at where a trace amount of blood is slowly seeping through the knee of my light-wash jeans. "Oh...oh, shit. Are you okay?"

"Yeah, um... I'm sure I'll be okay." I smooth over his soft brown hair. God, I just want to keep touching him and never stop again. "She's just at the apartment above the bakery."

He looks across the street toward our destination, then shrugs. "Let me piggyback you."

"Promise not to drop me?"

"Never." He takes my hand, pulling me to my feet, then boosting me onto his back. "I can't believe you quit. I mean, I *can* because you're incredible."

"Thank you." I breathe against the skin behind his ear, getting high off his musky scent and soaking up the warmth of his back as we cross the street. This is something I can get used to—traipsing through the tiny core of Fox Ridge with him.

"We're celebrating with the finest chicken tenders and fries tonight." Lucas sets me down outside the numbered door the realtor told me to use. And he opens it with a half-smile on his face. "You don't need your own apartment, you know."

I hesitate outside the entryway, seeking an explanation in his expression. The taut muscle in his jaw ticks, and he stares back without a hint of emotion.

"True. I could find a nice garden suite, or a carriage house, or a townhome." I tease him by ticking off the options on my fingertips. An insinuation isn't enough for me. If he wants me on his ranch, he needs to be a man and say it. "Oh, maybe a cabin in the woods?"

His mouth opens just as a woman's voice flits down the stairwell. "Ira? Is that you?"

"It's Eira," Lucas and I say in unison.

"Sorry about that! Come on up."

We follow her cheery tone—me hobbling at a painstaking pace, Lucas pressing a firm hand to my ass and preparing to catch me if I fall.

The initial glimpse of the space is beautiful—twice the size of my current apartment for a fraction of the price. I'd have no trouble affording this, even if commissions decrease for a period of time. Picture windows let in acres of sunlight, and the open concept carries that light, airy feeling throughout.

"Wow, it's gorg—"

"She doesn't want it." Lucas tightens his fingers around the shirt fabric on my lower back. "Sorry for wasting your time, Margaret."

"Oh, is there an issue with it?" she asks meekly.

"The issue is that it's not on my property, so we'll be spending a fortune on fuel going back and forth every day. Plus, I don't think her demon cat is going to appreciate the move."

I look at him, tears making my vision slightly blurry as they threaten to spill over. "Dolly at the shelter told me you didn't bring her in... You kept her?"

"Margaret—mind giving us a minute? Feel free to look around." He gestures to the space as if he's the realtor here, and turns to me, cupping my chin delicately. "Of course I did. My cat-sitting fees are astronomical, though. Especially when the creature is actively plotting my murder at all times. Plus, there's all the vet bills, her fancy canned food, and Band-Aids in bulk. You owe me big time."

"Thank you." In spite of my knee, I stretch up to kiss him, letting Lucas bear my weight in his arms. "Any chance you accept alternative forms of payment? I kind of quit my job yesterday."

"I'm actually in pretty desperate need of someone to keep my bed warm at night. And the problem is, I don't seem to have room there for anybody but you." He shifts his hold on my face slightly, tipping my head and running the pad of his thumb over my bottom lip. "Think we could work out a trade?"

I glance around at the perfect apartment that suddenly doesn't feel right at all. "Isn't this moving a little fast? Maybe we should live separately for a while, instead of jumping into things?"

"Are you saying that because it feels like you should, or because you want to?"

"Because isn't that the way relationships typically go? We date casually for a while, become exclusive, fall in love, and *then* move in together? This is everything in one fell swoop…" I look around at the vast empty space. All at once, it doesn't feel like a place that'll ever be home, but merely a stepping stone on the way to where I want to be. A stone I could simply skip right over.

"For me, everything already happened in one fell swoop when I saw you at the bar. Not love at first sight, per se, but familiarity. When you catch the eye of the one person you know in a crowded party and everything relaxes with the feeling of, 'oh, there you are. I've been looking for you'. Nothing weighs on you anymore." He presses a chaste kiss to the bridge of my nose. "That's how it felt. Whether meeting you was fate or coincidence or some damn good luck, I believe in it. I trust it."

I've been looking for you.

If asked to describe the night I met Lucas, that would be it.

"Margaret," I call out, not breaking eye contact with Lucas as we exchange smiles like a pair of love-drunk lunatics.

When she pops her head in from the master bedroom a moment later, I say, "Turns out I won't be needing your services."

"Neither will I," Lucas adds.

"W-well, but…" Margaret's eyes bounce between us with a confused expression. "Well, Lucas, what about—"

"Thanks for all your hard work, truly, but I won't be selling my place anymore." He smirks at my confused gawking. "Might be a little awkward if I ask my girl to live with me and then promptly make us homeless."

"Oh, okay. No worries at all. I'll go ahead and cancel the photographer and everything." Margaret pulls her phone out and taps away at it. All the while, I'm tugging at Lucas's sleeve like a small child demanding attention.

"Ready to go home, Doodlebug?"

Before he's finished the sentence, I'm halfway to the goddamn door.

"You were selling the ranch?" I grip his hand tight on the walk along the uneven sidewalk, taking careful, limping steps that don't require the full extension of my aching knee.

"Thought it might be time for a fresh start in the city." He shrugs casually. "I didn't want to tell you until it was officially on the market. That's why I couldn't come visit you—I had meetings with the realtor and lawyer."

With a shiver, I lean my head against his shoulder. "I'm glad I caught you in time."

"It was fate, baby."

Epilogue - Eira

One Christmas Later - December 22

Taking a step back, I tip my head from side to side, staring at this year's slightly misshapen tree. "Well, there's a bit of a bend in the trunk, so I don't think it's ever going to be perfectly straight."

"Okay, but"—lying on the floor, Lucas spins the tree base clockwise—"if we can get it to lean toward the window, it'll be less noticeable."

"It's perfect," I say, reaching out to brush a tiny icicle from a branch. "I can't believe I lived to see this moment."

Getting to his feet, Lucas combs a hand through his hair and chuckles. "Ah, yes. You were *so* close to death on the back of the calmest horse we have around here."

Unlike last year, Lucas and I went across the ranch on horseback to get a Christmas tree and dragged it like a sleigh behind his horse all the way back to the house.

I spent the summer taking riding lessons at the Therapeutic Riding Stables—*yes, I was in a class with six-year-olds*—and surprisingly, I feel pretty confident around horses now. No horse bites or other traumatic incidents. But that doesn't mean I can't remind Lucas how lucky he is that I survived each riding attempt.

"You never know. Maybe he's just playing the long game, waiting for me to fully let my guard down." I wrap my arms around Lucas's waist, settling into the crook under his arm and breathing in the scent of fresh pine. Half-Pint weaves between our legs, aggressively rubbing her forehead over our shins.

"Kind of like your devil cat is doing to me. She's patiently waiting to murder me."

"Oh, shush." I reach down and scoop her up, and she swats at Lucas's chest. No claw, though. *Progress.* "She loves her daddy, and you love her."

"Tolerate," he corrects me, giving Half-Pint a tentative head scratch.

Bullshit. This man insists on buying her the best wet cat food Fox Ridge has to offer and built her a *catio* so she can safely go outside after I mentioned being worried a wild animal might kill her.

"We should get decorating," Lucas says, slowly unraveling our intertwined bodies. "Mom and Dad are supposed to be here in the next couple hours."

I nod, setting Half-Pint on her plush bed and popping the lid off one of the decoration totes. "And your sisters are still coming tomorrow?"

"That's when the craziness really starts." He smiles, tugging a long strand of tinsel from the box. "Is it too late to cancel? I'd rather spend Christmas the way we did last year."

"Trust me, I'm already dreading having to wear pants on Christmas Day." I sink to the floor, a knotted ball of lights in my hands, and start meticulously working to untangle them. "It's a travesty."

Lucas takes a sip of bourbon before tipping the short glass to my lips. The liquid heat flows down into my stomach, instantly calming my nerves. Hosting his entire family for Christmas was entirely my idea, but why anybody actually let me go through with it is beyond me.

Lucas kisses the top of my head before clunking his glass on the coffee table. "We'll be pantsless from the minute they all go home on the twenty-sixth until January second."

"Perfect," I say. Both in response to his idea of spending an entire week without pants and because I've finally sorted out the mess of tree lights.

Just as last year, I focus on making sure the lights look perfect—and the tinsel garland is easily removable—while Lucas sorts through his childhood ornaments.

"I don't think I'm going to hang all these," he says, pursing his lips and staring at an adorable, tiny handprint moulded in clay. "I think we should just fill it with our own ornaments."

"Our *one* tree round from last year?" I laugh.

"Lucky for you, I got you a proper ornament this year." He smiles, holding up a small purple box. "If we keep adding to it, eventually we'll have a fully decorated tree."

I smile softly to myself imagining Christmas a decade from now, when we have a tote bin full of ornaments to reminisce and laugh and cry about together. A collection from every year, every vacation, every major milestone.

My fingers wrap around the dainty gold ribbon, and I pull out a small, ceramic cat figurine. With gold eyes and a mischievous look on its face, it's as if he had this custom made to be an exact replica of the kitty curled up by the fire right now.

"It looks *exactly* like Half-Pint. It's so perfect, Lucas. I love it." I throw myself into his warm chest, inhaling his comforting cologne. "Nobody is ever going to believe you hate her, you know?"

"This has everything to do with loving you, not her." Keeping an arm loose around my waist, he hangs last year's ornament at the same time I hang the ceramic cat, ensuring it's secure on a thick branch. Then we take a step back and admire our handiwork. Sure, the tree's a little crooked, and the tinsel could use some replacing after last year, and the branches are a bit barren...but it's perfect. Everything about this place is.

My life in the past year has become better than my best daydream. Commissions are booked out months in advance, and I'm volunteering at Fur-Ever Home multiple days per week. While the nonstop cabin bookings all summer had Lucas a teensy bit on-edge, the stress about potentially losing everything he's worked for is gone.

"Almost forgot... I had to get us another tree round." His hands are clasped together with what I assume is the handmade ornament concealed between them. And there's a sheen to his deep-blue eyes when they meet mine.

"It's tradition now," I state, attention cutting from his hands to his face and back again.

"Um... Doodlebug." There's a slight wavering in his voice, and he steps in to me. "Before I give you this, I just want you to know how much I love you."

"I love you, too." I wet my lips, squinting at his shaky hands, held fast around the piece of wood. "What's going on? You look worried. If you messed up the ornament or something, it's okay."

"No, no. It's not that. It's... This time last year, you turned my entire life upside down in the best possible way, and I don't know if I'll ever be able to fully show you how much you mean to me. But I'm hoping this is a start."

With a deep inhale and a rattling exhale, his hands slowly separate to reveal the perfect circle of wood cut from the trunk of our Christmas tree.

And a ring.

The twine used to hang the ornament is looped through the gold band. Neatly printed in sharpie on the wood are the words, *Will You Marry Me?*

"Lucas." My hand flies up to cover my mouth, and already there are tears blurring my vision. Frantically wiping to clear them, I find him waiting hesitantly on one knee. And suddenly I'm on my knees, too—grabbing his face in my hands and kissing him deeply. I mutter the word *yes* against his lips, into his mouth, so many times it doesn't feel like a real word anymore.

"I love you." The thumb of his free hand swipes at the rivulets running down my cheeks when we finally break for air. His forehead presses to mine, and I lose myself in his steady gaze.

"You somehow found a way to top last year's present," I say just before a sob racks my body. "God, how can you be so perfect? This is just... *the ornament?* I love you so much."

His bottom lip swipes over mine with the gentle brush of a kiss. "Baby, I think if your answer is yes, you're supposed to put the ring on."

Oh my God. Yes, yes I am supposed to do exactly that.

I give him my trembling left hand and watch the breathtaking pear-cut stone slide up the length of my finger. Then I kiss the man who's given me so much more than a cute ornament and a beautiful ring. What started as inspiration sketched across a bar napkin became a fate-guided masterpiece. He gave me courage, confidence, and a dream worth chasing. He gave me the one thing I never knew I needed: a perfect Christmas at Fox Ridge.

✳ ✳ ✳ ✳ ✳

If you enjoyed this story, please consider leaving a review!

Reader reviews are so instrumental in the success of indie authors. An honest review posted wherever you're most comfortable (Amazon, Goodreads, TikTok, Instagram, etc.) means the world to me.

And follow along on social media (@baileyhannahwrites everywhere) to be in the loop for my next love story.

Acknowledgements

Funnily enough, after I wrote a different novella earlier this year, I think I told every single person willing to listen that I would "never write another novella."

And then the moment I realized I had a small amount of free-time between projects, I started dreaming of Fox Ridge.

So thank you, most importantly, to my family for putting up with my inability to take a break. Maybe one day I'll learn how to take more than a couple weeks off from writing... *(I say knowing full well that I'll be jumping into the next project tomorrow).*

Samantha—I'm forever grateful some guy decided to send you a picture of his penis in a hotdog bun, and even more grateful that you let me write that story into a book. I love you!

Thank you to the incredible beta readers who are always down for anything I throw at them, even when that's a spur-of-the-moment novella. Abby, Amanda, Becky, Ceilidh, Chelsea, Danie, Maddy, & Sydney — you ladies are so wonderful to work with! Thank you for all the laughs, insight, and feedback to make this the story that it is. I'm blessed to have you all in my corner <3

Self-proclaimed *Queens of Wells Ranch:* I'm sorry I didn't insert a candy cane into any unsavoury places. Maybe next time you'll get lucky.

To my agent, Carly, for not questioning my sanity when, in the middle of all our work on the Wells Ranch series, I decided I was going to write this.

To all the ARC readers and incredible people hyping this book up before release. Thank you for trusting me and supporting my career, whether in the indie or traditional realm. It means the absolute world to me. My readers are the best readers <3

I hope this cowboy Christmas novella got you in the spirit for the holiday season. I hope you have a big teddy bear of a man to snuggle up with by the fire (or to tie you up in tinsel by the fire, if that's your jam). Most of all, I hope you had as good of a time reading this story as I had writing it.

Now be a good girl and go download some monster smut.

About the author

Bailey Hannah is a Canadian romance author with a passion for strong heroines and rugged men who aren't afraid to love their women hard.

Born and raised in small town British Columbia, you can count on a touch of rural Canadian flair (dirt roads, rodeos, and ketchup chips) in her stories. Bailey lives with her husband, daughter, dogs, and chickens. In her spare time, she enjoys reading, enjoying the outdoors, and daydreaming about her characters.

For the most up-to-date information on works in progress and other book news, follow Bailey on social media @baileyhannahwrites

Printed in Dunstable, United Kingdom